When the Leaves Began to Unfold

When the Leaves Began to Unfold

The Hurley Murder Mystery

Kim Hurley Andrews
and
Delila Mize McCabe

When the Leaves Began to Unfold: The Hurley Murder Mystery

This is a work of fiction based on actual events.

Library of Congress Control Number: 2025913624

ISBN 978-0-578-88924-5

Printed in the United States of America
1 2 3 4 5 29 28 27 26 25

First Edition: May 2025

On Facebook
When the Leaves Began to Unfold: The Hurley Murder Mystery

To order book copies, or for media inquiries:
kiminoz2002@yahoo.com

On the cover (from left): Faye Baker Self, Genevieve Pepper, Mollie Hurley Pepper, Thomas Andrew "T.A." Hurley and Ernest Hurley. Taken in front of the Hurley farmhouse, five miles southeast of Meriden, Kan., ca. 1915. Hurley Family photo

Photo of Lila McCabe courtesy of Chris McCabe Grandmontagne.
Photo of Kim Hurley Andrews by Kim Stahly.

For Gannon and Dakota. Grandpa Mike always said that you've got to know where you've come from, to know where you're headed.

—KHA

For Laurie, Dee Dee, Missie, Jerry Charles, Davie, Mona Lisa, Robbie and Dusty, and all who are to come.

—DMM

The Hurley Family

	born	died
Thomas A. Hurley (Father)	born 11-8-1837	died 5-14-1923
Mary E. (Mother)	2-19-1849	8-24-1914
1. Andrew J.	3-6-1866	12-15-1924
2. Maggie	8-11-1868	12-11-1946
3. Catherine	8-24-1869	4-18-1929
4. George W.	2-25-1871	8-27-1925
5. Hellen	5-11-1872	1876
6. Eli M.	12-20-1873	11-26-1959
7. Mollie	1-25-1875	8-30-1941
7(a). Mary (twin)	1-25-1875	1875/6
8. Libbie	4-5-1877	1-24-1964
9. Thomas J.	12-18-1878	9-21-1955
10. William H.	12-17-1880	3-1-1943
11. Jenevieve (sp)	2-8-1882	5-14-1923
12. Nora I.	3-5-1886	6-2-1972
13. Nellie M.	2-1-1888	5-19-1959
14. Ernest R.	9-1-1894	5-14-1923
15. Baby Stillborn	Unknown	

Taken from Family Bible
Aug. 12, 1914 by
Eli M. Hurley

(Death dates added by KHA.)

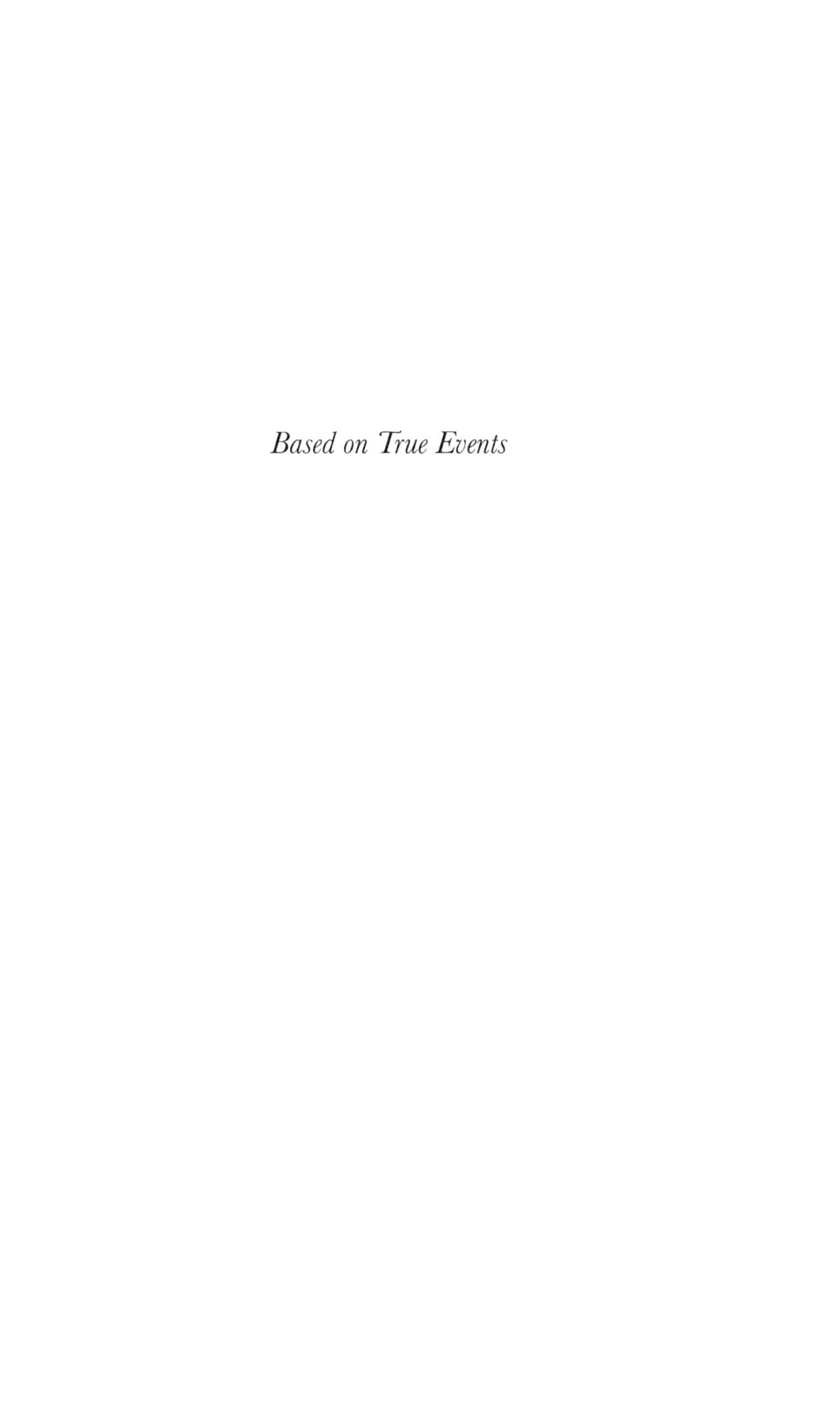

Based on True Events

CONTENTS

Oh, it's a beautiful day, such a beautiful day,
in this wonderful world we live in.
Just open your eyes, you'll realize,
it's a wonderful world we live in.

Don't grumble or groan, wail or moan
about the way that this world's run.
Just put on a grin, and start your day in
this wonderful world we live in.

—Song written by Lila McCabe,
sung by her and her grandchildren
as they came up the sidewalk to
Old Nate's house in Meriden, Kan.

Introduction

This book is about the unsolved murders that happened near a small Midwestern town in 1923. It remains the biggest mystery of Jefferson County, Kansas, and the surrounding communities of Meriden, Perry, Ozawkie and Oskaloosa.

One person lived to tell what happened that night. He was known as Old Nate. It's doubtful that he deliberately told a lie in all of his life. Yet Old Nate withheld evidence from the law, a secret in his heart for fifty of his ninety-three years.

At the center of the tragedy was Genevieve Hurley, known to all as Jennie. She was a beautiful 41-year-old Kansas schoolteacher. As Nate put it, she was "a looker." Any man would've been proud to have her as his wife, he said.

In this book, we will propose why the ring with a diamond as big around as the end of your little finger, owned by Jennie, was never found in the ashes of the Hurley fire. We will also bring to light the real tragedy of the Hurley murders.

How much of this story is true? Probably somewhere around 70 percent. Only a handful of characters were created out of thin air. Some names were changed. Many conversations were imagined. If something is not completely true, it likely has its roots in reality.

As Lila used to say, "Until you can tell a better story, let's just say this is how it happened."

BLUE VIOLET. —*Faithfulness*

Oh! there is never sorrow of heart
That shall lack a timely end,
If but to God we turn, and ask
Of Him to be our Friend.

WORDSWORTH.

From *Flora's Dial*

Part One

CHAPTER ONE

The Timber

1961

Thunder rolled off the black Kansas sky in swirls that echoed across the Delaware River Valley. On a hill in a thirty-acre timber, the old, tall trees creaked and swayed. A gust of wind passed over their tops, moaning violently, warning of an impending storm.

Underneath it all stood a tall, shadowy figure, a man completely drawn into himself, head bowed and hands clasped behind him. It appeared as though he'd closed a curtain around his soul.

Once, the timber had been his secret place. No one but the man himself was allowed to enter. However, something about Jennie Hurley earned his unflinching trust, and so he shared with her the precious knowledge of this peaceful place where the grass grew in long, soft shoots, a plush green carpet leading into an earthly heaven. Here, no one could harm him, no one could find him. No one, that is, except her.

She's gone; ah, she is gone. The reminder hit him with as much force as it did decades before. He clung to her memory desperately. Faithfully, she would return to him in sensate pieces that he carefully assembled in his mind. This was a constant struggle, not losing the grasp between them, that spanned light years. With every bit of anguished energy inside of him, with all the senses he'd ever been given, he remembered the very essence of her.

In his mind, he visually traced her round chin and impish nose. Heard her laughter ring out more clearly than church bells in winter. Caught a whiff of her sweet scent, which dizzied him whenever she passed. Reached out to touch her hands, so smooth, so white they were nearly transparent. Nothing could pull him away from her now.

He owned not a single photograph of her, and so he had to recreate her in his mind like this, over and over, or else she would completely disappear.

Over time, he established an evening ritual that was as necessary as stepping out of his worn overalls and crawling into bed. Night after night, for almost forty years Old Nate had come to this very spot in the woods. His vigilant footsteps wore a narrow path so smooth and reliable that he could walk into the trees, eyes closed, and end up in the same, strange spot without fail.

He always approached the timber from the south, where his one-room cabin stood near the road. It wound past a brome field before curving down into the valley—the Delaware River Valley—where she once lived. Nate would walk north into this field, instead of heading down the hill as he had on rainy evenings to be with her and the small household. He worked alongside Jennie's father and youngest brother, and called them his friends. Still, he'd rather admit to stealing horses than going down to the Hurley farm just to catch a glimpse of her.

A few moments after traipsing into the brome field, the top of his sandy-colored head would disappear beneath the horizon. Then once again, he would be with her.

There, in between two tall walnut trees, the ground sank a bit and the grass grew greener. His eyes closed in on a tiny clump of white wildflowers that blossomed each spring: *Erythronium Americanum.* Dogtooth violets. He knew this because he'd read everything he could get his hands on—encyclopedias, dictionaries, poetry books, fictional classics and, without fail, *The Valley Falls Vindicator.*

Old Nate's life was something of a puzzle. As intelligent as he was, the man had few words for his feelings. That is to say, what he felt was not what he projected; what lay beneath contradicted the exterior. And so, he could not tell Jennie exactly how she made him tremble inside, how he sometimes felt like the scared boy who slipped her a note in school one day, even before they met.

Because he could not voice this intense affection, he was destined to live a solitary life. The walls of his cabin represented visible barriers—wood chinked with dirt, sand and water. The less obvious ones were built around his soul. Although he hungered for stimulating conversation, someone to read poems to, and perhaps play a game of checkers with, he seldom spoke to anyone. The only person he let in his door was a man named Andy Petesch, who he paid to farm some of his land. Of course, Old Nate couldn't be beaten but sometimes he let Andy win, just the same. He liked Andy, and wanted him to come back and visit.

As he got on in years, folks began to call him "Old Nate." No one but his mother ever called him Nathan. He certainly didn't demand the respect that "Mr. Isaac" called for. People around Meriden, Kansas, knew him as one of those colorful characters who identified their town as much as a "Welcome to..." sign. After Nate died, his competition became a sailboat along the highway that bore these words: "Welcome to the Best Dam Site."

The legs of Nate's overalls billowed in the breeze like an old cloth sail. He wore the same pair day in and day out, seldom washing them. He shaved only when it suited him. His bedraggled appearance drew pity and sometimes fear. His leather boots were dusty and scuffed up, the toes curled on end. Perhaps if people had taken the time to get to know Old Nate, they'd see a man with unshakable strength, a logical mind and tender heart.

He was a creature of the darkness. Neighbors who passed by his place knew that when they saw him walking down the road in the evening, he was headed for the timber. Why, they could never quite say. They couldn't imagine what drew him back, night after night. It was as if a magnet were strung around his neck.

No one could guess Old Nate had a large wad of cash in the Meriden State Bank. Not even Andy, nor any of the other men who farmed his land. They knew he required little to maintain his needs: some chewing tobacco, which he went through by the sackful, and occasionally a new pair of overalls. When the denim got hard and stiff and smelled so ripe that even Old Nate couldn't stand it, he went to town, bought a new pair and buried the old ones in the ground. This could happen several times a year. And so, when the money from his farming kept coming in, it was more than he needed.

He owned a lot of land. True, it wasn't the best around, but that hardly mattered. Just as long as he owned plenty, was all he cared about. He'd buy and sell with the goal of improving his holdings a little each time.

So why did Old Nate seem intent on denying himself a comfortable existence? Some called the place he lived in a shack; he preferred to call it his cabin. He'd built the slant-roofed, one-room shelter himself. Measuring twelve by twenty feet, it allowed him to see from his front door the weathered barn where he kept his team of workhorses. Between the two buildings was a small valley. Along this ran a steady stream of water. Here, Nate washed his hands and face after a long day out in the field. Once again, his feet had worn a guiding path to this place, over time. This led straight down from his cabin, across the creek, and back up to the barn.

The cabin was stifling hot, most seasons. Old Nate stoked and coaxed the dying embers inside a coal-burning stove. Always, he could drink a cup of coffee. On winter mornings, his warm breath stretched across the room before he stepped out of his narrow straw bed. It sagged under the weight of two quilts his mother had started her marriage with, a half-century before. Many of the faded blocks were tattered and frayed, peeled back on two sides, revealing the cottonseed batting that provided little warmth these days. The blocks seemed to hold together sheerly through stubborn pride. Even when his mother and grandmother first pieced them together, they could brag of no beauty.

The heat of the cabin only heightened the aromas melding together. The smell of boiled coffee mingled with coal and Nate's simple diet of burnt bacon and overcooked beans. This permeated his clothes, allowing him to carry a reminder of home with him wherever he went.

For years, ever since she'd left him, he boxed himself inside the cabin. Yes, he tended to his chores, cared for his horses, plowed the fields and harvested year after year, but where he was on a deeper level was always someplace in between his soul and hers. His cabin, their secret place. Her home, before it was destroyed.

One day he would lay beside her, just like before. The longing in his heart cut a jagged place inside like a dull, rusty knife: toxic, with no hope of ever healing. This was the one thing he allowed himself to feel. Or, perhaps it was all he had room for. It left him with a bitter aftertaste, for he believed he had no hope of ever seeing her again.

Once he was gone, that was it, as far as Old Nate was concerned. He believed like Black Bart: "You come out of the dark, and when you die, you go back into the dark." Perhaps that's why Nate clung so desperately and eternally to his final remembrances of her.

Somehow, over his own scent he could detect the fragrances of the dense timber and the delicate dogtooth violets that grew there, still. How loyal they'd been to him, all these years. He merely put one foot in front of the other, closed his eyes, and it was as if they were together again.

CHAPTER TWO

The Storm

Something had gone terribly wrong, and it happened at just the right time. Just when he'd given up on ever sharing any part of her life, she returned to the valley. This time, though, two shocking blows: her mother's death, and the fact that there was little to say between them. All of her attention was focused on male callers who came from the city and drove her away in shiny automobiles: Packards, REO's and sometimes, Benzes. Not a plain black Model T in the bunch. More fancy than anything Nate had seen or could hope to own.

She wanted style and class, whatever exuded wealth and status. Certainly he couldn't woo her if it took a long, dark coat, a pair of clean, white gloves, a custom-made Woolf Brothers' suit, and enough wax to finish off a mustache in two near-perfect rings. He'd seen such men come and go as he stabled the cows for the evening with her brother.

"Quaint." It was on their lips as soon as they stepped out of their mohair velvet-upholstered seats and onto the dusty ground. Waiting for them were a farmhouse, a barnyard full of geese, and chicken manure, which sometimes spotted the soles of their polished shoes as they made their way to the boardwalk. This had better be one grand dame they'd come to fetch. And grand, she was.

Years after the tragedy, as he held onto the secret inside, Old Nate would continue to repay himself, deny himself, believing he deserved no comforts, no convenience. Of course, he didn't recognize his behavior for what it was, a mirror of the life he'd experienced as a child. His parents had pulled him out of school early to do more important things, namely, work. He would never tell anyone, but he was embarrassed by his mother's loud voice and cloddy hands, and his father's reputation for using a six-shooter to settle arguments. Then there was the fact that his dad had climbed on top of a manure pile next to the barn when he realized it was his time to die. It was as if he were saying, "This is what life has been like, for me."

Tobacco was the only luxury Old Nate allowed for himself. Quite often, he would be holding a good-sized plug in his cheek. He liked to sit in his rocking chair and spit at the cockroaches and crickets that darted across the floor. When he'd hit one, he'd wipe his mouth with the back of his hand, sit back in his chair and smile in satisfaction.

Whatever conclusions people drew about him were usually wrong. They couldn't guess the reason he worked so hard and covered the palms of his hands in blisters and callouses. When he went out, he wore a gray-striped engineer's cap. On humid days, the inside got dark and soggy, and his hair was pressed down in a temporary indentation. In back, it jutted out like stiff forks. He was a strong man for his advanced age, but his muscles were beginning to atrophy. The skin on the inside of his arms hung in loose folds.

As Old Nate stood there in the timber one evening, the sky began to darken. It looked as if a curtain were being pulled across the horizon. A few minutes later a lightning bolt flashed, brightening his face. His body glowed eerily. Instinctively he dropped to the ground. Immediately after came a crack so loud that his eardrums nearly burst.

One of the oldest, most statuesque walnut trees in the timber split clear in half, all the way down to the roots. Old Nate lifted his head just in time to see one side of the tree fall, hitting the ground with a shudder. It bounced and landed across the creek. Another riff of lightning lit up the sky, adding a punctuation mark. Then an angry voice seemed to roar above, shaking the entire Delaware River Valley. The deep rumble extended like an uninterrupted line of cursive writing.

Nate's ears were ringing, and so he couldn't hear the soft telltale sounds of the approaching rain which mimicked cicadas in the distance. As he stood, the first few drops of sky-felled water kissed his face. Rapidly it turned into a cold, slapping-down rainpour. Nate leapt to his feet and began to run up the hill. Big drops splattered the earth, bending leaves and grass with sheer force. When he reached the brome field, the approaching storm was clipping at his heels like a hunter intent on a kill. The wind was bending to the northeast saplings that had been sown haphazardly by blue jays, wrens, meadowlarks and whip-poor-wills. The tilled rows filled with water before he could reach the end of the field. Then he disappeared into the trees.

A flattened bed of leaves down by the creek revealed where he had knelt, awaiting doom. Here, a new growth of stringy green prairie grass emerged; in the middle was a tight, natural bouquet of dogtooth violets. They shimmered brightly, covered in rainfall. Someone could have mistaken them for a handful of scattered diamonds. But who would dare to leave something so precious in the forbidding timber?

CHAPTER 3

A Last-Ditch Effort

"Whose bright idea was this dam?" A burly farmer, his plump second chin covered with as much dark stubble as the first, demanded to know. The brim of his red-labeled seed cap was intentionally broken to form an upside-down vee. A flat brow served no use to a man who worked out in the weather.

A hundred and fifty other farmers, their wives, the Jefferson County commissioners, some bankers and other businessmen gathered in Ozawkie at the town meeting hall that evening to protest the proposed dam. The Corps of Engineers was set on carving up the beautiful, fertile Delaware River Valley.

Another man bellowed from his place against the wall. "I don't know, but I'd like to give those fellas a piece of my mind!" Years of farming told on his face. His wife discreetly tugged on his shirtsleeve to prevent her embarrassment.

"I'd like to point out the fact that whatever we decide probably won't matter a hill of beans." The presence of a well-known banker hushed the crowd as he took the floor. He was wearing the same suit he'd put on that morning. By the looks of the creases in the back of his jacket, he'd been sitting in a chair most of the day. "You've seen signs posted across the county on all the telephone poles and in the store windows," he went on. "They've already pushed through Congress the legislation and funding to make this happen. There's no stopping them, now."

The meeting hall was packed with folks who were desperate to keep their farmland. For decades the Corps of Engineers had talked about putting in a dam and flooding much of the area. "A damn bunch of foolishness," folks called it. But this time, it looked like it just might happen.

It happened right under their noses. A truck would come to a sudden halt out in the country, and two men would get out and unload a wooden tripod and rod. One would peer through a telescope mounted on the tripod and adjust an instrument called a *theodolite,* invented three hundred years before, by an English mathematician. Underneath a scope, in the center of the tripod, a conical-shaped piece of metal pointed toward the ground, hanging from a string. Many yards away but within the first man's eyesight another man stood, holding the wooden rod with measurements printed on it.

Only the most intelligent people could be surveyors. Using geometry and trigonometry, they measured triangles in a way that allowed them to plot land elevations and contours. In Jefferson County, all this was preparation for figuring out where the lake should stretch out from the Delaware River and across the land. They were planning to cover the rich valley with miles and miles of water.

Folks at the meeting that night could care less about how much schooling it took to map out their precious land. All that mattered was protecting it. They'd heard the government's propaganda from specially trained representatives who staged informational meetings that only served to muddle the situation. Tonight was the citizens' night. If they were going to do anything, now was the time.

"I say we appoint someone to let those government types know that we're not going take this sitting down," another farmer leaning against the back wall said. Every chair in the house was taken. Many people stood with arms crossed.

"You know we'll be lucky to get anything close to what our land is worth," one man asserted. The crowd started murmuring.

A gavel pounded the podium. "Let's hear what this man has to say," a commissioner demanded.

"I have a brother who farms outside of Manhattan. He says this looks like what happened to them, not long ago. They fought, too, but what good did it do? Everyone got a lowball figure, about a third of what their land was worth. Took some hard-nosed negotiating. Then they got less than three months to bring in their crops and get out of there. I'd advise everyone affected to hire a good attorney."

Another commissioner stood up. "All right, folks. We'd be lying if we said we weren't concerned about what's ahead. Some of us have heard stories about how they go in with bulldozers, plow up everything and even knock down utility poles. I don't want to sugarcoat it. It's probably going be a nightmare before it's over. Just keep in mind that this could take years to happen."

"They're pushy, too," the last farmer who spoke, added. "If you drag your feet settling with them, they'll move those bulldozers in and burn everything around you, just to get you shook up. With all that noise going on, I'd be calling and agreeing to a price, too!"

"I am not moving. No sir!" another said. "They can burn everything I own, including me and my place. I'll never leave!" Others nodded in agreement.

"It's not like this flooding problem is new," the first commissioner said. "We've struggled with it for years. Our dads and their fathers lost crops every year because of it."

"Why do they have to do something so drastic as create a permanent flood? Why can't they just plant grass to control the runoff water?" a farmer suggested.

"How about putting in some farm ponds and terraces?" another offered.

"What we've done, until now, is like putting a cork in a big bottle," the banker explained.

Heaven knows they'd tried to keep the waters from filling the valley. Half a century before, farmers working the bottom land hitched a steamer to a diking machine and pulled it four miles down Rock Creek to the Delaware River, then three more miles down the Delaware. It worked for a while, but over time the dike eroded. Once again, the land along the valley washed out. Along with it, stalks of new growth and unrealized dreams were stripped from the soil.

"What will happen to Ozawkie?" someone asked.

"They're figuring on taking about fourteen thousand acres, or a quarter of the county," one of the commissioners, Claude Brey, answered. "That's where it'll start, and I'm afraid there won't be much of it left."

"But the men from the Corps of Engineers said they'd only take the land on the outskirts of town," one woman tried to correct, her voice nearly breaking.

"I'm sorry, but no," Brey revealed, hesitantly. "I'm afraid that's not in the final plans. If you're lucky enough to keep your land, you'll probably get saddled with paying off the project bonds."

"You mean we'll have to pick up everyone else's tax bill?"

"Yes, ma'am. It'll be spread among the remaining landowners."

The crowd murmured and almost turned to protest. "Not if I have anything to say about it!" one cried.

"How could they even think of that?" another said, shaking his head in disbelief.

"That's the problem," Brey said. "They don't seem to care. And unless we go up there and talk to them in their Washington office, they'll think they can run over us and do whatever they please."

"Just what are you proposing?" the first farmer asked.

"I'd be willing to go up and talk to those officials," Brey offered, "but I need your support. I've got to take something to them that says the rest of you feel the same way."

"We sure as heck do!" a man chimed in. The crowd responded with hearty applause. "How about a petition? That's how we've taken care of things in the past."

"I'm all for that," Brey agreed, and others followed, until it was determined they needed an official vote.

"All in favor of appointing Claude Brey to take a petition up to Washington and speak on our behalf?" one of the commissioners asked, raising his hand. Every farmer and their spouses did likewise.

"Anyone opposed?"

No one dared to vote against the last-ditch effort to save the Delaware River Valley. Not even those who suspected it couldn't be done.

CHAPTER 4

The Near-Miss

Old Nate should have been at the meeting that night. For his entire life he'd lived in that one small corner of Jefferson County. Now, at age 83, he was in danger of losing everything. Eunice Petesch knew this. Old Nate was all she could think of, as she and Andy made their way home from the meeting that night. Andy's thoughts were turned toward the sky and some big, impressive clouds churning above. They seemed to hang right over their '51 Hudson Hornet.

"I don't like the looks of this a bit," Andy said, clutching the steering wheel tightly. "See those clouds?" he said, frowning. "We just might get a tornado."

Up from the timber, their car headlights cut through the darkness, lighting up the road a hundred yards or so. Andy rolled down the window for a closer look. Rain splattered dark spots on his hat. Eunice squirmed beside him. "Not to worry you, dear, but be ready, just in case we need to get out of the car," he warned.

An approaching storm, combined with warm, damp air, could possibly form a twister from out of nowhere. If two opposing wind forces melded together, it could create a vacuum that scooped down into the countryside, lifting barns, cattle and trees. It could spin them up and hurl them miles away. Homes and outbuildings standing in such a great funnel's path could be torn into pieces as it sucked up and pulled away the earth. Even paved roads were no match for the strongest tornadic winds, which could rip the dark, bituminous ribbons from the ground.

That was where a tornado met the earth. Alongside it was hazardous enough. Here, high winds with as much speed as a hurricane and hail up to the size of baseballs or grapefruit could wreak enough havoc to move buildings off their foundations, uproot trees, and cut through roofs and windows.

Andy and Eunice had farmed the fertile Delaware River Valley for a solid forty years. Like most Kansans, they'd grown accustomed to keeping an eye on the sky. Dangerous spring weather was the relative who came for months at a time and quickly wore out its welcome. They simply gritted their teeth, crossed their fingers and prayed. If their homes were destroyed, they'd clear away the debris and probably rebuild in the same spot, knowing it could happen all over again.

Just a year before, a tornado had come up from the southwest and wreaked havoc on nearby Meriden. Scores of houses and buildings were destroyed but only one life was lost. The town was still in the midst of recovery and vowed to come back even stronger.

By this time, the rain had covered the ruts on the gravel road. Andy maneuvered the car around them as best as he could. Township roads like this received little maintenance. The last thing he wanted was a flat tire. This was no night to get out and jack up a car.

Just then, something darted in front of them. "Andy, look out!" Eunice yelled.

Using all his strength, Andy stomped on the clutch and brake at the same time. The steering wheel shuddered; the car skidded across the road. "Son of a gun!" Andy hollered, his hat smashing up against the ceiling. He ground the gears into neutral.

"My word!" Eunice yelled. "What was that?"

"I don't know!" Andy exclaimed.

"Was it a deer?" Eunice asked.

"No," Andy said, shaking his head. "Too tall."

"Looked like it was standing up. Maybe a man," Eunice offered.

Andy peered out into the timber. "Maybe a bear," he joked nervously, trying to reassure her. Then he put the car into gear and headed down the road.

"Whatever it was," she said, "between that and the storm, I'm downright spooked. I, for one, will be glad to get back home. We could have hit it, Andy," she supposed.

"But we didn't," he reminded her.

"What if it was a man? Who'd be crazy enough to get out on a night like this, in the middle of a pouring-down rain?"

"Practically everybody we know was there tonight, in Meriden," he pointed out.

"I know one person who wasn't," Eunice said so low that he could barely hear her.

"Who?"

"Old Nate." She shot him a sidelong glance. "I've been thinking about him ever since we left that meeting. Did you see him there tonight?"

"Nope. But I wasn't looking for him."

"Looking for him? You know you could have just smelled him if he was there. Besides, if he wanted to go, wouldn't he have asked for a ride?"

"Probably. Guess he stands to lose a lot if this lake comes in. Bet the water would cover up all of his bottom land."

"Then doesn't it seem odd that he wouldn't bother to show up?"

"You know he doesn't like to be around a lot of people, Eunice." Andy wasn't convinced they'd seen Nate in the road. Just what it was, he couldn't say.

"Maybe not, but it seems like a fella ought to take some interest in a meeting that could turn his whole life upside down. He loves this land. It's all he's ever had. It's all he's ever known." Eunice turned toward him and kept making her point. "And how many times, just how many times have we driven down this stretch of road, Andy, and seen Old Nate heading out into that timber, or walking the opposite way like he's headed back home?"

Andy didn't know if she was onto something, but for Nate—or any man—to be out in a night like this seemed, well, a bit crazy.

"What do you suppose Old Nate does when he goes out into that timber?" Eunice asked, suddenly curious.

"Probably just talks to the birds and squirrels. They'd be all the friends he's ever had, I suppose."

"They say he had a lover once."

Andy forced himself to keep looking straight ahead.

"Say what you want, but that's what I hear," she answered his silence.

He decided to play along. "So tell me, Eunice, who was this lover of Nate's?"

"This is going to be hard for you to believe, but...."

"Go ahead. Give it a shot."

"Some say it was Jennie Hurley."

"Genevieve Hurley? That beautiful, middle-aged woman who died in the fire? From the way people around here talk about her, she had way too much class to go after someone like Old Nate. Besides, everyone knew she was engaged to Lon Myers."

"Lon was a farmer, just like Nate."

"But he was respectable... and normal."

"And comfortable, as far as money was concerned."

"Bingo, Eunice. That's why Jennie would marry him. Always had big money in mind."

"More than any of the boys around here, had."

"Meaning…."

"Meaning, it was just as strange for her to be associated with Lon Myers as Old Nate," she explained. "In our eyes, Lon was higher class, but to Jennie he would've been just another sod-buster."

"Who'd she want to be with, then?"

"Those rich city fellas. Ones who drove big, expensive cars. But I guess there was a time when she and Nate did like each other."

"Genevieve Hurley was sweet on Old Nate?" he asked.

"I think they were good friends who grew up together. Maybe Nate was different then, more friendly."

"Must've been, because I can't see him wanting to be around any woman."

"Remember that lady who took him a pie?" she asked.

"You mean the one who said he threw it on the ground, right in front of her? Best cherry pie maker in the county. What a waste!"

"Old Nate vowed to never care about another woman after

Jennie Hurley died. Or so I hear."

"She was something to look at." Andy clucked his tongue without thinking, then attempted to roll it back. "Or so I hear."

"It's no wonder Nate chased after her."

"Even a dopey kid like me knew better than to run after girls who wouldn't give me the time of day," he said, putting a new angle on the conversation.

"You chased me."

"Only because you wanted me to."

"I did, at that." Eunice smiled and softly touched Andy's face. "Well, you don't know. It could've happened."

"What?"

"Nate and Jennie."

"Ah," he discounted. "School chums, maybe. But lovers?"

"So what do you think Nate does, out in that timber?"

"Maybe he's got a still back in there, and goes out to take a nip, now and then."

"Don't be ridiculous. Nate's not a drinker."

"Just thought I'd throw that in, since the conversation's getting pretty silly. Even you admitted a man would have to be a fool to stand outside in a downpour... no matter how fine the liquor."

Eunice smiled and shook her head.

"He probably just wandered down into the timber and got caught in the rain," he supposed.

"But his cabin isn't that far away. You'd think he'd run back before the storm got so bad."

Andy rolled his eyes. "Eunice. Why don't you just leave well enough alone?"

She sat in a pout, arms crossed. Then she asked, "Andy, just how long you been farming for Old Nate?"

"Years. A decade. Maybe more."

"And after all this time, you still don't know him. Not really."

Old Nate was fortunate to have been born and raised in the most beautiful part of Kansas. If one had to stay all his life in one place, this was it. For all its trees, hills and winding roads, Jefferson County looked more like Missouri. There were forests or timbers of hickory, ash, elm, hackberry, walnut, maple, oak and cottonwood trees. Before he came along, there were large orchards of apples, peaches, plums and berries east of the Delaware River.

If Nate ever wanted to leave and explore the world around him, he could've boarded a train at Valley Falls. (The town was originally called Grasshopper Falls until a plague of grasshoppers came in, more than once, and stripped everything clean that was green.) Or, he could've departed at Rock Creek, Meriden, Nortonville or Nichols. Steam locomotives from as many as six railroad lines trudged through the county over time, their stacks burning clean, white smoke when the fireman worked hard to shovel coal into the firebox, and gray when he was slacking off or short on fuel.

"If the lake comes in like they say, all this land up here could be worth a thousand dollars an acre, maybe more." Andy was sitting at the kitchen table reading the latest issue of *The Vindicator*, which led with a front-page article about the protest meeting in Ozawkie, earlier that week. The leftover egg yolks on his plate were beginning to harden.

"No!" Eunice turned at the sink, where she was washing dishes.

"Yes, ma'am." Andy nodded thoughtfully from behind the paper, then handed her his plate. "Says in an editorial, they think lots of people will move in and build nice, new homes so they can spend their weekends on the lake."

Eunice raised an eyebrow. "Not anybody I know."

"They'd be outsiders. Folks from Topeka, Kansas City, even farther away," he said, waving his hand for emphasis.

"Might bring in more tourists and businesses," Eunice supposed.

"Might even stop all the flooding," he added sarcastically.

"It's just so hard to imagine all this wonderful farm ground covered by water... on purpose. How come you didn't say more about this when we came home from the meeting, Andy?"

"You were wrapped up in Old Nate's love life. Besides, the government will do whatever they want, no matter what any of us says. Anybody asks, tell them I don't like it a bit. Hate to say it but we might have to move, before it's all over."

Eunice scowled. "What makes you think so?"

"They've got a little map, here in the paper. Can't be sure, but if we don't, it'll be darn close."

"If we have to move, Old Nate will, too."

"Reckon so."

"Oh, I hope not, Andy. That would just about kill him."

"He'd adjust. Like the rest of us."

"But Andy, he's never lived anywhere else. It'd be like trying to uproot a big, old tree. His roots run deep! You'd have to cut him out of the ground. Even if he moved someplace nice, he'd probably just wither away and die."

"Eunice," Andy chided. "For starters, anything would be an improvement over that old shack of Nate's. And besides, he's made of strong stock. There comes a point when a man's got to do what a man's got to do."

CHAPTER 5

At the Bank

Clay Alderson was perspiring so heavily that the back of his tan work shirt kept sticking to the front seat of his '56 Chevy pickup as he drove down Main Street. He barely stopped in time to pull into a parking place in front of the State Bank of Meriden. His front tires smacked against the curb, giving the truck and everything inside of him a shudder.

White paint was peeling off the grain elevator. An imposing structure, it rose from the background and reigned over the block-long downtown. Only one of thousands that stored golden treasure cultivated each summer, its unmistakeable presence towered above the town, revealing that the county's prosperity lay just beyond the city limits.

A block from the co-op was a two-story limestone building. Here, the Masons met to strengthen their relationships and perform ancient rituals steeped in Old Testament scripture. The ideas were nothing new, touting a life that was full of integrity. Each man vowed to come to another's aid in times of need.

Directly across the street was the post office. On this day, it seemed as though you could reach out and wring water from the air. Bathing seemed pointless; by the time a person dried off and got dressed, they were damp again. It was the kind of a day that made everyone wish they lived somewhere north, somewhere cooler. Of course, when the wind blew snow across the brick-lined street and folks had to fight to keep their hats on, they'd wish for this day again.

The secondhand swept past 9:12. The young banker, Daryl Becker, had been at work for half an hour, admiring two antique rifles he'd picked up at an auction over in Tonganoxie the weekend before. Someday he hoped to have the best Winchester collection in the state.

Blond and smooth, Becker would've made the perfect political figure had he chosen to get into the fray. He was articulate and well-educated, with a relaxed style that put people at ease. He pulled a new hard pack of Marlboros from his pocket and tapped it on the glass that covered his dad's walnut desk. The Beckers were an old Jefferson County family who'd seen all that four generations could endure.

A cloud of ashes rose from the trashcan as Daryl dumped the remains of his conversation yesterday with Old Nate. It lasted more than six cigarettes because Nate could never directly say what he wanted. Daryl always set aside twice as much time when the odd bachelor came in. This time, Nate wanted to sell him some of his mediocre farmland. It was a pretty piece of ground, but he couldn't find anyone gullible enough to farm it for him any longer. He knew Daryl had his sights on building a house there, so Nate figured he could just about name his own price.

"All right, what do you want for it?" Daryl said, rolling up out of a relaxed position from his brown leather chair to look eyeball to eyeball with Nate. The bachelor tugged on a tobacco-stained string tied to the bib of his dirty overalls. He pulled a plain silver pocket watch out of the front pocket, looked at it, rose silently and started walking out of the office.

Daryl slammed a hand down on his desk. "Nate Isaac, get back in here! You want twice as much as it's worth?"

The thought of dollar signs and commas rang through Nate's head like a cash register bell. He returned to his chair and smiled slightly.

"We both know I'd be a fool to give you that much, but I can meet you somewhere in between. Something we can both live with." Daryl shot him a conceding look from under his eyebrows. Nate had him cornered but there was still a little wiggle room. Daryl circled his pen above a yellow legal pad, deep in thought. Then he dared to mark down a figure, and slid the pad across the desk. "How's this grab you?"

Nate twisted his face. Was it a grimace, or was he trying to hide a spontaneous holler of joy? Instead, he sucked down a piece of loose phlegm, making a sickening sound. Then he nodded.

"All right. Let's get these papers signed. That's what we came here for, isn't it?"

Later, Clay Alderson peered through the bank door. Before his eyes had time to adjust to the light, Daryl was waving him back to his office.

"Morning, Mr. Becker," Alderson called warmly.

Daryl grabbed his hand and shook it. "Glad to see you, Clay. What have you got going on, today?"

"Thought I'd bring you some of the new surveying we've done. It's going be a beauty, once this lake goes in." The excitement rose in the young man's throat. There was nothing more invigorating to him than conceiving of a new state park and watching it come to life. Sure, Kansas wasn't the place he'd hoped to end up, but it was a step that could take him farther west, where the hills were steeper, the forests deeper, and the land less willing to be tamed.

"So this lake project is finally going to happen, after all?" Daryl asked casually, hoping to reel in a new bit of information.

"Yes, sure is."

"You know, this isn't the first time we've had surveyors running all over the county, talking about flood control projects."

"I understand. And I can appreciate folks being hesitant to believe it, but this time, it's for real."

"So, where you been working, lately?"

"On up north." Clay unrolled a map to show him.

Daryl noticed how the shaded area for the proposed lake intersected with the town of Ozawkie. "Well, that won't work," he said. "You've made a mistake, there."

"Why is that?"

"This shows water running right over Ozawkie."

Clay looked at Daryl, then blinked twice.

"You're not mistaken, are you?" Daryl whispered.

"Nope, afraid not."

"Oh my," Daryl said, reaching into his pocket for a cigarette. "Please tell me you're joking. Claude Brey said he thought so, back at the citizens' meeting, but I was sure he'd gotten ahold of a wild tale."

"Like I said, I wish I wasn't, but this is the only way. It's right where we're going to put in a big bridge that stretches more than a quarter of a mile."

"What'll happen to all the folks up there? Some of that land includes cemeteries, you know. People who've been buried there since before the Civil War."

"I have to tell you, this certainly isn't the most pleasant part of the job. You just can't expect to put in one of the largest bodies of water in Kansas without shaking things up. For the most part, it's going to involve farmland. But this is an area where we just can't compromise."

"Anyone else know about this?"

"The guys who staked out the land with me, and my supervisors."

"You'll be even less popular when word gets out."

"You'll give me a running start, right?" Clay joked. They both laughed. "At least I'm not the one who has to deal with these people and give them the news in person."

"Who's helping you?"

"About a dozen fellows from back East. One of them is named Becker."

Daryl stopped in the middle of inhaling his cigarette, and sputtered. "You're kidding me."

Clay smiled and shook his head. "No. Sure am not. Sounds like you'll have some explaining to do, these next few months."

"Months? How about years?"

CHAPTER 6

Just a Little Inside Info

Claude Brey went up to Washington and did his best to convince the government that putting in a dam was just too drastic. Paul Cawley of Valley Falls, and Casey Dick and Glenn Lehman of Ozawkie accompanied Brey on this enormous task. Together they sat in on the hearings before a committee of the Engineering Division of Rivers and Harbors, part of the War Department. Brey reasoned that another dike could temporarily solve the flooding without disrupting the entire county. Planting tall grasses might also help, he suggested. But in the end, the bureaucrats were unmoved. Their decision remained final: Perry Lake was going in, whether folks in Jefferson County wanted it, or not.

The project was estimated to cost a thousand dollars per acre. The Corps of Engineers would build a dam on the Delaware River, five miles north of Perry. At fullpool or flood stage, the water would run back into a reservoir running a mile north of Valley Falls. In the end, it would take $47.9 million and five years to transform the countryside into a monumental, man-made lake. It would only displace one old cemetery, on the south end: the Olive Branch. Graves would have to be moved to a new location. Some of them were members of the Hurley and Metzger families.

"Morning." Daryl Becker flashed the government man a guarded smile. "You must be the one we've heard about, who's coming to buy all the farms for the new lake."

"That's right," Chuck Becker acknowledged nervously, wishing he'd worn his boots. This would be the only office visit on his schedule today, and his brand-new dress shoes wouldn't take kindly to dirt and weeds. Just what he'd gotten himself into, he wasn't quite sure. Underneath his arm was a rolled-up map with a rubber band.

"I guess you know we're related," the Easterner said succinctly.

"How much are you paying an acre?" Becker dismissed. In no way did he want to be connected to this man.

"Not nearly as much as it'll cost the War Department to put in the lake," Chuck flipped back.

Daryl scowled. He wanted some concrete figures so he could advise his customers—not dodges and well-constructed explanations. People would soon be standing in line at his bank with questions, and he needed as much info as he could gather.

"At this point, I really can't say," Chuck went on, sensing Daryl's irritation, "since I'm not allowed to disclose that, yet. Of course, if your land were on my list, that would be another matter."

"You won't find my name on it. At least I hope not!" Daryl chuckled, trying to break the tension. He was one of the fortunate few. His land was several miles west of the project. Then again, if he'd thought far enough ahead when the talks began, he could've bought some of the land himself and potentially made a profit.

"So what can I help you with?" Daryl redirected.

"Before I get started, I'd like to see if I could get some lowdown information. Like to do my research, first."

"It's a little inside scoop you're looking for?" Daryl was tempted to hold back, since Chuck was being evasive. However, his conscience quickly won out. Besides, if Daryl wanted any precious details, he'd have to earn the stranger's trust. "What do you need, specifically?"

"I need to know who will go easy, and who won't. Easiest way to convince them, of course, is to put a check in their hand, and then ask. Harder to resist after they've seen all those figures. Younger folks are the easiest to persuade. They almost never question. Don't have the money to hire a lawyer, either."

Daryl would remember this when his customers came in. "Hope you're up for the challenge," he said bluntly.

As soon as Chuck sighed, he knew he'd blown his cover. Didn't matter how many towns he walked into, they were all the same: innocent people living innocent lives. He was about to strip it all away and remind them rather coldly that they weren't the captain of their own destinies. Usually, it was better if he just didn't think about it too much. After all, he was only doing his job. "Surely you can give me a sense of how these folks will respond," he finally softened. "They are your customers, after all."

"And neighbors," Becker reminded him. "Some, for several generations. So you want to know which ones will cooperate, and which ones could be tempted to fill your backside with buckshot?"

"Something like that."

Daryl wanted this meeting to end quickly. "All right," he said, motioning for Chuck to put his map on the desk. Daryl sat a brass paperweight down on one end before leaning over the county map thoughtfully. He'd seen it countless times. Only next time they printed it, there would be a large gaping hole in the middle. "Where you planning to start?"

"Straight east of Meriden, about here," Chuck pointed. "Then south, into Perry."

"For the most part, you shouldn't run into any real problems until you get to this section." He pointed to a piece of land marked "Isaac," then smiled wistfully. "How much they paying you?" he asked. "Around here, this guy is known as Old Nate. Never lived anywhere outside of this circle, his whole life. Doubt he's ever stepped foot outside of Jefferson County."

"Really?"

"Keeps to himself. Doesn't cause any real trouble, but he's plenty strange. Lives alone in that old shack of his. No running water, no electricity."

"He's not a danger, then?"

"Probably not, but he also won't put out the welcome mat for you. He's stubborn, for sure. Very peculiar about that timber north of his cabin."

"Timber?"

"Big grove of trees next to a creek. The kids who play nearby say they see him out in it a lot, especially when it starts getting dark."

As Nate drove his team of horses up the hill road, the evening sun cut through the trees and cast shafts of hazy light across his shack. The road wound between his place and where the Hurley house once stood. The harnesses on his horses jingled wearily. This pair of roans had been Nate's constant companions in recent years.

He thought fondly about the Hurley family every time he passed the sprawling large maple tree out front of their place. He thought of Thomas, a well-respected, stocky old Irishman whose height seemed to increase several inches whenever he entered the doors of a Meriden business. There he would announce in a deep, loud bellow, "I'm T.A. Hurley from Rock Creek below, and I'm the biggest damn sheep farmer in all of Jefferson County!"

When the rain soaked the fields, Nate would ride his horse down to the Hurley farm for a satisfying dinner prepared by Jennie. Nate, Thomas and Ernest would take turns shoveling down generous portions of beef, pork or lamb. Always, there was a big bowl of mashed potatoes whipped so thick the serving spoon stood straight up. Freshly snapped green beans or shucked corn ears glazed with butter sat on the side. A sweetened batch of strawberries and shortcake topped with cream was a favorite dessert.

Jennie insisted on the civility of finger bowls filled with warm, lemony water before and after each meal. The men obliged her strange city habit, dipping the tips of their large hands into each glass bowl that sat near their plates. At the end of the meal, they wiped their hands and wadded up the starched and pressed linen napkins. Jennie carefully refolded hers. She'd taught school nearby before landing a premier position in the Kansas City, Kansas, school district as the director of music. Toward the end of her time there, she accepted invitations to dinner parties at the country club and drinks at a speakeasy, where live music and watered-down liquor never ran dry.

This sharply contrasted with her new life, once again on the farm. Jennie spent her days fixing meals and washing dishes or laundry. In the evening she played piano while Ernest and Nate hunched over a checkerboard. She'd returned after her mother's death, which also happened to coincide with a misunderstanding between her and the school superintendent.

Ernest and Nate ended a checker game and leaned back in their chairs. Ernest put his hands between his shirt and tight overalls, trying to gain another inch of space for his expanded belly. The men laughed as Jennie shook her head at them.

"You two are like a pair of young hogs! All you need is to go outside and find a nice big mud puddle to wallow in. Maybe I should go upstairs and see if I can find a pretty bow to tie on your tails. Then you could go out and find two decent-looking sows to marry."

"I've already found someone," Ernest said, winking at Nate.

"Put on a suit and tie once in a while, and you might catch something worth bringing home," she said snidely.

"I dress up for lodge and church!" he protested.

"And when does Nate ever clean up?" Jennie asked.

The pair looked at each other, puzzled. "Weddings and funerals," he said. Together, they burst out laughing. "That's it!" Ernest said, pointing at Nate.

"Okay, you two, get out of my dining room and go sit out on the back porch."

As they walked through the parlor, Nate snuck another peek at Jennie, noticing every line and curve, especially her fine, white hands and well-kept nails. He caught her eye just as she turned to go back into the kitchen: they were dark and deep set. By evening, her luxurious crop of brunette hair wound up in a bun would begin to fall loosely, leaving a few wisps to brush her cheeks and neck.

Nate's eyes grew misty. In an instant his mind was transported. He could see her move from the back kitchen door, out to the side yard, where she stood next to the clothesline, fighting the wind to hang a sheet. His ability to remember everything was sometimes a curse; it reminded him that she was really gone.

He led the horses across the grass, now damp with fresh evening dew, and into the barn. Once they cooled off, he'd wipe their coats dry with wisps of straw, then finish with a brush. Next, he'd lean down and rub their tired legs, checking the hooves for stones. Anything caught between the shoes could turn them lame by morning.

Nate built the barn so the stalls had dirt floors that sloped gently. Each were about six feet wide and sectioned off with wood. At the head of each stall was a manger. Here, Nate would dump some oats, their usual dinner, followed by hay. Once the horses were settled, he'd go back to his cabin for a bite to eat, then return later to clean the horses and their stalls. Only then would he retire for the evening.

Nate took his usual walk down to the creek between the barn and his shack to wash up. He paused to breathe in the clean, evening air before dipping his grimy hands in the cool water. On this evening, a silent figure stood on the path leading in from the dirt road. He couldn't make out who this was, since the setting sun only revealed an outline. It made him wonder. No one ever came to see Nate unless there was business to take care of. He could just about guess, though. He took off his hat and slapped cold water on his face.

"Mr. Isaac?" a voice called from the path. Nate stood there as the stranger slowly approached. "Name's Chuck Becker," he announced. Close enough now, to greet the old man, Chuck reached out his hand in friendliness. Nate ignored the gesture.

"You related to Daryl Becker?"

"No, sir. My folks come from back East. You know they're planning to come in soon and start working on the new lake?"

Nate nodded.

"Well sir, I've been hired by the government to come pay you for your land. Just need you to sign this form, so I can give you the check." Chuck pulled out a clipboard. Nate, with his face still dripping, wiped his hands on the front of his overalls.

"It's the same offer we sent in the mail," Chuck said, pointing to a five-figure amount. "Since you didn't answer our letters, I had to come talk to you in person. If you'll just sign here, I can be on my way."

Chuck handed him a pen. If Nate took the offer and signed, it meant he'd agree to quit claim on his land and vacate the premises. It was a lowball amount. He should've asked Daryl Becker for help. He wasn't about to hire an attorney, and Daryl did a fine job handling most of his legal work. Nate looked for something to balance Chuck's clipboard on. "Bend over," he instructed the young man.

Chuck looked at him in disbelief.

"Bend over, boy. I need something to write on. You want me to sign this, right?"

"Why, yes," Chuck answered, a bit confused. He leaned over and rested his hands on his knees.

Nate put the clipboard on Chuck's back and scrawled his name on the bottom line. Then he stuck Chuck's pen inside his overall pocket.

"Here's your copy," Chuck said. "You get the pink one. And here's the check. You can cash it at any bank in the county."

"It'll go in my bank," he replied quickly, then turned and walked away.

Before Chuck could gather himself and realize his hands were shaking, Nate was already halfway back to the shack. "Thank you, sir. Good day to you." He stood there, frozen. At the least, he'd expected the old man to ask for more money.

Nate went inside, closed the door, ate a few beans, drank a little boiled coffee, peered back outside to make sure the stranger was gone, then went out into the timber. When he was through talking to Jennie, telling her just what had happened, he returned to the barn to put away the horses for the night.

Like every evening, he stepped out of his overalls, hung them over the rocking chair, turned down the kerosene lamp, climbed onto his cot, covered up with his mother's quilt and slept until dawn. Another day, just like the next. Except his predictable little world had just been changed in ways he couldn't begin to imagine.

For months, Nate had thought about what he'd say to the unlucky soul who'd hand him that check. At first, he was angry. Nate planned to live here until he died, and now they were taking that away. However, he was a realist, and knew they'd probably build the lake whether he wanted them to, or not. *Better to go with a shred of dignity,* he thought. Better to have some peace of mind than to let it eat him up inside.

He liked to keep people guessing. So, if Old Nate didn't react at all, people would truly wonder. They would be surprised to know he was already planning to move into town. Someone told him that Gene and Nellie Huber's two-story house in Meriden was for sale, along with all the furnishings. That would be something, he thought: to live in the house where two of his favorite people had lived.

They had been a part of his life for a long time. Nate left his home when he was just a boy, carrying a dime in his pocket. He didn't get far, and stopped when he got down to the Hubers. In exchange for his labor, they gave him a comfortable place to sleep and plenty to eat. It was some of the best food he'd tasted. The Hubers were a generous couple who donated land west of the Delaware River for a school that later bore their name. It was the same school Nate attended, where he first met Jennie Hurley.

Like a circle, Nate was going back. Never mind it was a different house in a different location. It was still Gene and Nellie's place. By living there, he would feel them everywhere around him. The house in town had been well taken care of. And so, even before Old Nate knew the asking price, he decided to buy it.

CHAPTER 7

With Calloused Hands

Why everyone didn't wear denim overalls was beyond Old Nate. Most comfortable thing to wear, besides a nightshirt. The only other clothes he owned were a few work shirts, some cotton, some flannel—all wrinkled, most of them pretty threadbare—about four pairs of dingy socks which he layered in the winter, long undershorts that came two in a pack down at the dry goods store, a pair of work boots, and two pairs of sturdy gloves.

He made everything last longer. When his boot soles wore thin and his socks got wet, he put a few playing cards in the bottom. When that didn't work anymore, Nate drove down to Mike Weber's Shoe Repair in Valley Falls. Mike did fine work at a cheap price. Inside the shop, the rich aromas of leather, saddle soap and mink oil hung in the air.

Mike was trimming a thick strip of rubber to form a new sole. Nate leaned on the wooden counter, resting his hands under his chin, fascinated by all the footwear lining the shelves. A dull-looking pair of cowboy boots leaned to one side, a pull strap torn at the top. A two-inch heel was gone from a woman's purple suede shoe. A pair of shiny wingtips looked like they had seen too much pavement in their lifetime.

"Sounds like that lake is going in," Mike said, searching for an awl on his workbench. Nate barely blinked. Mike peered over the top of his glasses. "Guess it won't be so bad."

Nate tugged on the dirty old string hanging from his overalls and pulled out his watch: 10:30 a.m.

"Take about an hour or so," Mike said, anticipating Nate's question. He knew that most of them went unsaid. "Got to get this pair of boots ready for Charlie Winters by 3. Coming over on his break," Mike said, pointing toward the shelf. "You know, Charlie thinks people from all over the state will come to camp and fish at the lake. Says it'll bring in more business."

Nate remained silent.

"I can sell you a piece of leather for the watch," Mike said, trying hard not to stare at the old string. "Only fifteen cents."

Nate shook his head and left.

At the co-op, two metal gas signs hanging on a light pole banged against each other. Three pickups were parked in the gravel lot. A handful of men stood at the counter with their hands in their pockets, laughing as Nate walked in.

"Then old Mueller grabbed a sack of feed and said, 'I don't care if my stud thought Harrison's gelding was a mare!"

One of the men put on a jacket that bore the distinctive blue and white co-op emblem. "What can I do for you today?" he asked.

Nate pointed up at the green chalkboard hanging on a wall. Someone had drawn perfect white circles on it. Lines connected each circle. This was the layout of the elevator, showing where different grains were stored and how full each concrete silo was, by percentage.

"Wheat looks good so far," one of the men said. "Maybe some of the best in the last few years. They ran out of room yesterday, but with the storm last night, things oughta slow down for a while."

"Need anything else?" the co-op man asked.

Clearly, Nate was getting in the way of their conversation. He walked over to the leather goods that hung on a rack and looked over a bridle.

"That'll run you five bucks."

Two men at the end of the counter looked at him. "Hey, aren't you the fella that won the corn-shucking contest last year?" one asked.

Nate nodded.

They raised their eyebrows. "So, what's your secret?"

Nate shrugged.

"If he told us, he wouldn't need to bother entering again, would he?" one of them joked.

"Hey, you've got a point there," the youngest said with a laugh.

Holding a plug of tobacco in his mouth gingerly, he looked to be about 15 but was trying his best to fit in.

"Can't you give us a hint?" one of the men asked.

Nate grabbed the boy's baby-soft hands and shook his head. "Have to be tough enough to cut with a knife," he said.

The boy looked up at Nate, puzzled. He slapped the boy hard on his back. The youngster swallowed the tobacco and coughed. All the men laughed as the boy darted out the door and threw up in front of the store.

"You've got to have one hitting the buckboard and one in the air while another is in your hand," Nate revealed to the older men, gesturing with his hands.

"At the same time?" one of them asked in awe.

Nate nodded, then darted out the door, leaving the group to speculate whether he was telling the truth. As he got into his truck, he saw the boy outside wiping his mouth with the back of his hand. Nate tipped his hat in acknowledgement and drove away.

Inside, the men were still talking. "Isn't that the fellow Bob McGarity talks about? The one who rammed a piece of wood clear up through his wrist?"

"Sure is," the eldest said. "That old boy is Nate Isaac. The way Bob tells it, his dad was shucking corn with Nate across the road, north of Nate's shack. A team of ponies pulling the wagon ran wild, and Nate grabbed the reins to stop them. About that time, his arm grazed the side of the wagon, and a splinter at least six inches long rammed all the way up through his wrist."

The teenager, who was back inside, looked mortified. Perhaps he'd go back outside and throw up, again. "What did he do?"

"Well, his immediate reaction was to yank it out. Should've bled to death out there in that cornfield."

"But he didn't," one man noted.

"No, because he reached down and slapped some axle grease on it."

"Dirty old grease?" the youngster asked, in disbelief.

"You bet. Tough old guy, ain't he?"

CHAPTER 8

A New Home

Charles McCabe and Lila Mize fell in love and married before Lila was 18. Soon after, their first daughter Jody was born. Then came Lanny and Chrisie. Both Charles and Lila wanted the best for their girls. They didn't want them to grow up in hard times, as they had known. Charlie walked to school barefoot. Lila and her siblings were sent to an orphanage when the State decided their mother couldn't take care of them. The time spent imprisoned with the cold, abusive women who cared for the children left a mark on young Lila. She was sassy, and fought back. It was a good thing, for it kept her and her siblings together.

Lila sang to her younger sister in the orphanage when she was scared. At night, she would put a sheet or blanket on the floor when she heard the girl crying, and scoot on the floor from her bunkbed to her sister's. Then she would hold her hand and comfort her until she fell asleep. A smile and a song, and lots of love; that's how they survived. And one day, they were finally reunited with their momma.

As Charles climbed the rungs of a major cigarette company, driving across country and supervising salesmen, he and Lila were able to provide well for their children as well as others who came from less-than-ideal families, or had none at all. The McCabes often opened their home to the abandoned, abused, disabled and misunderstood. Lila more than Charles was open to this, perhaps, but even the tall man with the booming voice couldn't resist a child standing next to him, patiently waiting to be picked up and held.

The McCabes were working on building their first home on twenty acres north of Meriden, known as the Tripp Place. When they'd built as far as they had money, someone suggested this: "A body might ask Nate Isaac for a loan; he has most of the money in the county."

With all of her heart, Lila wished that she and Charles could finish their lovely home. They were working to rebuild after the tornado. She asked someone where this Nate Isaac lived, and drove out to his cabin. As she pulled up and watched him carry an armload of wood, it cast a memorable picture. The sun was setting behind this man who had idea no why she'd come, nor who she was. The image and moment lingered in Lila's mind all of her life.

"What can I do for you?" Old Nate called out to her, squinting in the near darkness. Lila's confident stride reminded him of a woman he once knew.

"Someone told me that you had a lot of money and might be willing to loan some of it," she announced boldly.

Nate wasn't accustomed to folks being so forthright with him, but he liked it. In fact, he admired it. But he should never let her know, he decided in that moment. His face grew somber. Lila followed him up to his shack, where he unlatched the door with an elbow. "I never make a practice of loaning money to anybody," he said without turning.

Her eyes widened. She was taken aback. "Why, I'm sorry to have bothered you," she apologized. "I imagine someone's laughing at me, about now. Seems as though I've been the butt of a cruel joke."

Nate dumped the wood on the floor. "No hard feelings?"

"Certainly not," she replied, feeling embarrassed and disheartened.

"You lived around here a while?" he asked, trying to make her feel better.

"Yes, over in Meriden," she said.

"I'm moving there, myself."

"You're leaving this nice little cabin? Why, it's such a pretty place to live!"

"Haven't got a choice," he explained.

"Oh, the lake. I see. Well, perhaps we will meet again another day."

"Perhaps," he said. "Sure we haven't met before?"

"I can't recall as though we have. Why?"

"You seem mighty familiar."

"Could be that you know my mother, Edith Orr. She cooks for the school children in Meriden."

"Can't say that rings a bell. She look like you?" In what appeared to be a reflex, he looked down at Lila's dainty white hands. Then he suddenly closed the door between them.

Lila, somewhat dumbfounded, turned and walked to her car. *Strange man,* she thought. *And me, out here all by myself.*

Nate thought about Jennie as soon as he shut the door. *I could buy you the diamond ring you always dreamed about, Jennie girl, as big around as your little finger. Now I'm buying a house in town, just like you always wanted.*

The move from his shack into town would be easy. Most of the things he owned were in the barn. No point in keeping them. It pained him, but Nate sold his horses along with the tack.

What will it be like, to live in town? he wondered. Certainly, he couldn't go out into the timber every night like he'd done for the past thirty years. He'd come back again, he promised himself. Would the dogtooth violets still bloom if he weren't there to see them? Or would they wait until he returned?

The Huber house was just as he remembered. Still had the same familiar, warm scent of fresh sheets and home cooking as he recalled from his visits there, before the couple died. Soon, the smells of Old Nate's bacon and boiled coffee would mingle with it, and the only two places on earth where he felt at home would seem like one.

He gathered his books, a woolen blanket, his daddy's freedom quilt, a dented pan, a few pieces of silverware, a lamp and an aluminum coffee pot, and put them all in the back of his old blue pickup. He ground the gears into reverse, backed out onto the road, slammed it into first and never looked back.

As he wound his way up the hilly country road, he passed the place where he'd been born. It was nothing more than a caved-in pile of wood. Then he drove by the little white Huber schoolhouse where he learned to read and first spied Jennie across the room. He stopped at the highway, then drove onto the newly paved road leading into Meriden.

When Nate got into town and pulled up in front of the house, he walked all around, checking the foundation. It looked sound. The roof wasn't in bad shape, either. In all practicality, he should have checked things over before he signed the papers. However, because it was Gene and Nellie's, he would have bought it anyway, even if it were in a state of disrepair.

He sat down on the front steps. This was his home, now. No more shack. No more farming. No more government men on his doorstep. No more nightly visits to the timber. His stomach gnarled inside. The night before, he'd fallen asleep out in the woods, knowing it would be his last visit for quite some time. So long as the timber wasn't underwater, he'd find some way to get back.

Nate reached out to pull himself up, and the object he grabbed was of no use, for it simply swayed back and forth: the front porch swing. Funny, he hadn't noticed it when he drove up. So many years had passed since he and Gene had sat on that very swing together, talking about farming, watching the sun set over the neighborhood.

Gene and Nellie moved to this house when they retired. Gene told Nate he didn't care much for town life but there were a few good things about it. Trying to remind himself what Gene had said, Nate sat on the swing and looked up at the eyebolts that anchored it into the porch ceiling. He gazed out at the neighborhood. Jennie had once been his neighbor but they lived so far apart that it wasn't within hollering distance. Nate hoped his new neighbors weren't noisy, and that they settled in early, at night.

Besides tobacco, the swing was the first unnecessary thing he owned. Jennie would have enjoyed sitting there, swinging gently and talking away the hours. *If only you were here,* he thought. As the sun began to fade away into dewy darkness, a robin sat on a tree stump in the front yard and began, as Nate used to say, to "preach him a sermon."

Old Nate on his porch swing, at the Huber's former house in Meriden. Here, he dreamed of the days with Jennie, and Dee Dee put the silver watch chain on his overalls, and he cried. Photo by Lila McCabe

Like the lilting of a favorite hymn, he heard the gentle laughter of a girl from across the street. It took him back to the schoolyard where they played tug-of-war and Annie, Annie, Oxen Free, and the special afternoons he walked Jennie home, past his house a mile.

That night he tossed and turned, trying to get used to the unfamiliar surroundings. He covered his head with the blankets, attempting to silence the noisy memories banging away in his mind. Finally he succumbed to sleep by early morning, as a lone bird began to sing. He dreamed he was in the timber with Jennie. It was May, just as the leaves were beginning to unfold, and the dogtooth violets were in bloom.

Nate slowly grew more accustomed to his life in Meriden, away from the shack and timber. He made a habit of sitting on the post office steps in town. There, he chewed and spat his tobacco, wiping his chin with the back of his hand when the dark brown spittle didn't make it all the way to the ground.

The postmistress, Agnes Dawber, passed Nate on her way into the brick building each morning. One day, as Nate sat with his head bowed, contemplating the world as it passed by, Agnes rudely kicked him in the leg. "Why don't you go home?" she badgered. "Don't you know we don't want you hanging around here?"

Looking up at her through gray, wiry eyebrows, Nate thought, *Who died and made you queen of the U.S. postal system?* Nate wasn't bothering anybody. More than anything, he was bothered by her interruption. He'd been thinking about Jennie. She'd done some mean things in her time, but Jennie wouldn't have kicked anyone.

He remembered how Mary, Jennie's mother, took in weary strangers passing by. Some would call them hobos, these people who had no home. She would give them a hot meal and a comfortable place to rest along the way. One of them drove a plain wooden stick in the ground at the end of their driveway. This was the universal sign that needy travelers gave each other to say they were welcome. Later, someone else carved a large wooden cross and stuck it in its place to let others know this was a Christian home, a safe and generous place to be.

Most folks didn't notice Nate as he sat there on the post office steps. He didn't want their pity or friendship and preferred that people left him alone. Certainly Agnes or anyone else who looked down on him didn't succeed in intimidating him.

Then the little woman who came up to his shack, asking for a loan before he moved, passed by. "Did you get your loan?" he called out to her.

"Hi there, Nathan Isaac," Lila answered cheerfully. "How is everything in your world?"

"Just fine," he said, spitting tobacco juice on the ground next to him. "Just fine."

Lila didn't think about Old Nate again until November, when she and her family gathered for Thanksgiving. "We should take some of our food and share it with others who might not be so fortunate," Lila's mother Edie said, after grace was offered. Edie lived just down the street from Meriden Grade School, where she served in the lunch line.

"Let's fix a couple of plates and take one to old Bart, and that old fellow who just moved into the Huber place," Lila suggested.

"Which fellow is that?" her husband Charles asked.

"You know… the one who had to give up his land for Perry Lake," Lila explained, trying to remember his name. "Nate Isaac. That's it."

When they were done eating and started cleaning up the kitchen, Edie fixed two large plates. She piled them high with turkey, mashed potatoes and gravy, dressing, cranberries, homemade bread, and pumpkin pie with whipped cream. Lila took it upon herself to deliver the dinners. She invited her grandchildren along for the walk. They went to Bart Archard's, but he wasn't home. They figured he must've been invited somewhere to a Thanksgiving dinner, so they left the plate sitting on a front porch chair.

The five children's heads bobbed as they skipped and sang

down the sidewalk: Dee Dee, Laurie, Missie, Jerry Charles and David. As they got closer to Nate's, they saw the old man get up from his swing and go into the house. Lila thought this a bit odd. The group trudged up the steps and knocked on the door. There was no answer.

"We've got Thanksgiving dinner for you," Lila called. The children echoed her, enjoying a crazy game of repetition.

Nate opened the door a crack. "Take it away!" he bellowed at her. "Take it away, I said. I don't want any!"

"What do you mean, you don't want it?" Lila scolded as if she were his mother. "It's good food, and it costs money. We're going to leave it here on the swing, and don't you let the dogs eat it!" she ordered.

As they walked away, Lila looked behind her. The curtain pulled back a little. Nate peeked out at them. Later that evening, Lila and her grandchildren returned to check on the plate. It was still on the porch, but all the food was gone. "Maybe a dog came and ate it all up," one of the children supposed.

"No, it's been scraped clean with a fork," Lila noted with satisfaction as she got closer. "Old Nate had himself a Thanksgiving meal, after all."

Lila wondered about the old man. *Who took care of him? Did he have any family? Did he eat every day? Was he in good health?* She hated to see folks in need.

When the McCabes were leaving for their vacation that summer, Lila decided to take a loaf of homemade bread to Old Nate. She'd baked a batch and didn't want it to go to waste. This time, when Lila offered him food, Nate reached out and took it. Then he bowed a gentlemanly thanks to her.

Edie Orr went back to cooking for the schoolchildren and realized that almost every day there were leftovers. She remembered when nothing could be thrown away during the Depression, and it bothered her to toss out perfectly good food. She tried to give it to her grandchildren but they weren't excited about eating the same meal twice a day. *Surely someone else can eat this,* she thought.

When Lila learned that Nate was a bachelor, Edie sent her over to his house with a small pan of leftover spaghetti. Just in case the old man refused, Lila was ready with an explanation. She decided she wouldn't take no for an answer. "You're a bachelor and have no one to cook for you, Nate," Lila said before he could hardly get the door open. "And besides, this food is just going to go to waste unless you take it."

Nate reached out and took the little pan from her.

"If I knew you'd take more, I'd keep bringing it to you," she said. Silence passed between them. "How come a good-looking guy like you never got married?" she asked with a twinkle in her eye.

"Because I never had a rubber-tired buggy," he answered gruffly.

"Ah, but a good-looking fellow like you wouldn't need a rubber-tired buggy!" she jested, hoping to lengthen the conversation.

"Oh yes, I did, and by the time I got one, all the desirable women were spoken for."

Lila walked down to Nate's almost every night to bring him supper. Sometimes she'd bring along her grandson Jerry Charles. After a while, Nate trusted the pair enough to invite them into his house. They were his first visitors. Lila spotted a checkerboard in the corner. "Do you play?" she asked.

"Why, yes."

"How about a game?"

"I'd like that," he responded.

Jerry Charles sat down in a big chair beside old Nate and fell asleep.

"Did you know Jennie Hurley?" she asked. Lila had heard about the local tragedy that took the life of a woman, her father and brother, decades before.

"Yes," he said tersely.

"Was she pretty?"

Nate was slow to answer. Lila wondered if she was prying too much. "Jennie... was a looker," he answered softly. "Any man would have been proud to have her as his wife."

Like most folks in Jefferson County, Lila was fascinated by all of the details about the family's suspicious deaths and the fire that burned down their farmhouse. Some were rumors, some were true. It was such an intriguing story that *The American Weekly*, a Sunday magazine published by William Randolph Hearst and inserted in major newspapers across the country, chronicled it in a full-page spread a couple of years later. There, all the way across the top, was a drawing of Jennie Hurley, depicted as a 1920s flapper, replete with a bobbed hairdo. She was dragging a body, draped in a sheet.

Nate had actually known Jennie Hurley. Lila was intrigued. Perhaps he could tell her things that no one else knew. However, she was careful what she asked. One false move might break his trust, and she didn't want their new friendship to end. "You know about the fire?" she dared to ask one day.

"Of course," he answered quickly. "Everybody knows that story."

Lila felt she was beginning to break through with him. She found out that her granddaughter Dee Dee and Nate shared the same birthday: February 27. When they visited him on their special day, the little girl crawled up on his lap and hung a new silver watch chain around Nate's neck. It replaced the old tobacco-stained shoestring. With tears in his eyes he thanked them, then patted Dee Dee gently on the back. It was the first birthday present he'd received in years.

"What time is it, Nate?" Lila asked with a smile. She watched him pick up the new chain to look, and saw a tear run down his cheek.

Lila returned one day to Old Nate's with clean bed clothes. She wanted to replace the rough, dirty canvas sheeting that usually covered his mattress. She found him in the middle of a checkers game with Andy Petesch.

"What you got there, Lila?" Andy asked. The Petesches and McCabes knew each other through community activities.

"Oh, just some clean linens," Lila answered, then headed upstairs to make Nate's bed.

"What's she up to? Are you planning to invite a woman to your bedroom?" Andy teased.

Nate clenched his jaw and fists, then suddenly stood and stormed the stairs. When he reached his room, he pushed Lila aside, tore the clean sheets off the bed and threw them into a corner.

"Why Nate, what on earth are you doing?" Lila asked. Just when she thought she had him figured out, she was confused again. Still, she kept coming to offer help.

Another time, she took one of Old Nate's shirts to the laundry. When she brought it back, clean and fresh smelling, he took her hand and squeezed it. "Will you come back tomorrow?" he asked. He loved to recite poetry with her. And there was always a game of checkers to play.

It seemed like everyone was afraid of Old Nate—except Lila. One day when she was there, someone came to his door. Two boys in crisp Scout uniforms stood outside. "Who is it?" he called. "No, I don't have any newspapers!" he hollered to their shocked faces. Lila rose from a chair. "Nate, you have stacks of them!" she scolded. "You boys come right in and get them."

Jerry Charles liked to wander through Nate's house when she brought him with her. The boy never bothered anything, so Nate didn't mind. In fact, he liked Jerry Charles. He gave him some old marbles and pictures to take home.

One day, Jerry Charles stopped in front of a small desk. He opened a drawer and pulled out a small pistol. Nate glanced up from his checkerboard. "Put that gun down, boy!" he roared. Jerry Charles startled, dropping the pistol back inside.

"What's wrong with you, Nate?" Lila scolded. She got up and

looked at the small weapon. "Why, it doesn't even have a cylinder in it."

"Get out, get out!" he barked at them, pointing to the front door. "And don't you come back!"

Lila pulled Jerry Charles to her side, and left.

Days passed. Lila missed Nate and their checker games. She wrote a poem for Nate called "Beloved Senior Citizen":

I want somehow to please you,
Though I never know just why.
I want to make you happy
Many times before you die.
It seems I'm forced to worry
About the daily things you do.
It's though a power within me
Says please watch over you.
It's more than putting joy into
Your dear old, lonely heart,
It's more than showing kindness,
For it's a pleasure on my part.
Could it be your mother's soul
Was reincarnated into me,
And she's asking me to cheer you
Till this old world sets you free?

A few days after she mailed the poem to Nate, Lila saw him sitting in his usual place on the post office steps.

"Where you been?" he asked softly as she walked by.

"Oh, around," she tested, wondering if he were still angry.

"Why haven't you come to visit lately?"

"I didn't think you wanted me to."

He dismissed her feelings with a wave of his hand.

There would be more checker games to play. Lila washed Nate's dishes, took his laundry, and promised to return the next day. "Was

Lila at the age when Old Nate told her the story about Jennie.

Dee Dee, age 3.

The bunch that came singing down the sidewalk to visit Old Nate: top, Lila and Jerry; center, Laurie, David and Missie; bottom, Dee Dee.

Laurie, age 4.

Dee Dee, when she put the watch chain on Old Nate. Her birthday was the same as Nate's—February 27.

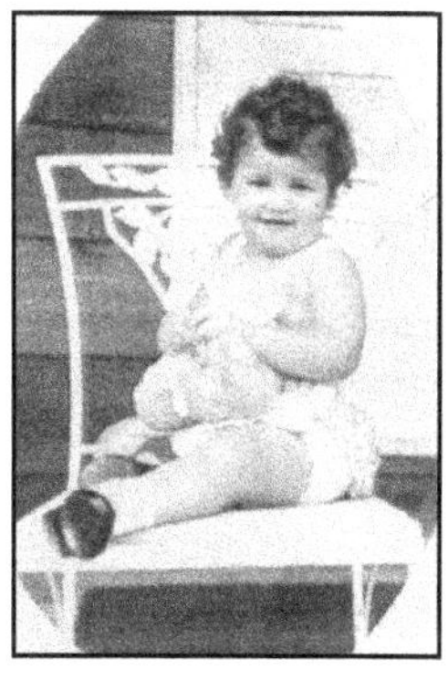

Missie, age 2.

Photos from Lila McCabe

Jennie Hurley your lover?" she asked, when the trust was strongly rebuilt between them.

"I'd like to think so," he replied.

Charles started coming to Old Nate's house with Lila, cutting his hair and shaving him while Lila read the newspaper aloud. The three of them drove over to Brown County, where Nate looked over some land he'd bought with the check the government had given him for his Delaware River Valley land.

There, Jerry Charles climbed up into a barn. As Nate saw him heading for a robin's nest up in the stanchions, he gave a gentle warning: "Don't bother that nest, boy. I'm rather fond of that bird."

"It sure would be nice to build out on the new lake," Lila commented.

"You mean that old mud hole?" he said with a laugh.

"Sure."

Nate shook his head. "Tell you what: I'll trade you my lake land for your wheat land in Meriden, acre for acre."

"But Nate, your land must be worth five times as much as ours! Besides, what would you do with a bunch of wheat land?"

"Doesn't matter."

"Oh Nate, are you sure?" She was elated by his generous offer. "You'd make Charles and me so happy!"

They all rode over to Oskaloosa the next day and closed the deal for a dollar, each. It was the same land that he had bought from Gene Huber for thirty dollars an acre.

Part Two

CHAPTER 9

Roughing It

Jennie's father, Thomas Andrew Hurley, was only 14 or 15 years old when he left Cork, Ireland, around 1850 and stowed away on a ship bound for America. So the family story goes, that was handed down.

Like all Irish immigrants, Thomas sailed to England before getting on a larger ship. And then, his Transatlantic voyage only happened after he proved himself healthy enough. (That is, if he went through proper channels and didn't stow away, as some claimed.)

When the second vessel landed in America, according to family, young Thomas found work on the Erie Canal. With a couple of other young Irishmen he purchased a team of oxen and a covered wagon. Together they crossed through forests and prairie to reach Colorado. There, he sought fortune along icy river banks, peering endlessly into the bottom of a gold pan.

Thomas made his way back east to Kansas before the Civil War, driving a freight wagon on the Military Road between Leavenworth and Meriden. At the fledgling town called Easton, he stopped to water his team. Here, one day, he met Mary Metzger, only 8 years old. She had come from Pickaway County, Ohio, with her parents Eli and Harriet Stout Metzger, grandparents John and Margaret Zimmer Metzger, aunts and uncles, and cousins. To this day Jefferson County, Kansas, and the surrounding area is filled with their family.

A year or two earlier, the nearby town of Lawrence had been sacked by pro-slavery settlers. Lawrence would experience more conflict and grief in 1863, when a schoolteacher named William Quantrill and a band of almost five hundred Confederate guerrillas attacked one morning. They killed more than one hundred men and boys, burning most of the businesses.

Like many area men, Thomas enlisted in the Kansas State Militia. In October 1864 he went to Oskaloosa, the county seat, and became a part of Company B, Fourth Regiment, under Capt. Golden Gilbert, who answered to Col. W.B. McCain.

Thomas' company, composed of thirty-five men, traveled east to Kansas City, Mo., where they joined up with four hundred Union soldiers. At Westport and along the banks of Brush Creek (now Kansas City, Mo.), they battled Gen. Sterling Price's rebel troops. The fighting lasted a couple of weeks. Two or three men in Thomas' company were captured in the battle but escaped as Price's men were driven south. The entire company returned to Jefferson County without harm.

The week that President Lincoln was shot, Thomas and Mary rode together on the back of a horse twenty-six miles to Lawrence and were married by a Roman Catholic priest. They settled in Jefferson County, not far from the Military Road, on what is now the banks of Perry Lake, close to D.J.'s Rock Creek Marina. (Much of their farmland is presently covered by water. A parking lot near the Corps of Engineers office is on the south end, where Thomas had a hog lot.)

The first year of their married life, a plague of grasshoppers ruined all the crops in the county. Thomas likely grew up on a farm back in Ireland and understood the typical unpredictability, but this was something he'd never faced—a reminder that he was subject to all the glory and devastation that God allowed.

Their first child, Andrew Hurley, was born a year later. Mary had been raised a Lutheran but honored Thomas' family tradition. She and the infant were baptized in the Catholic church one blustery Sunday in October. Little Maggie came into the family next, then Kate. Both received the same sacrament.

About this time, Mary's 13-year-old sister Barbara arrived to help care for the house and children. The two sisters looked very much alike, it was said. According to census records, the unmarried Barbara bore a child in 1870. At the time of its conception, a 32-year-old boarder named Tom Robinson also lived with the

Mary Elizabeth Metzger Hurley and Thomas Andrew "T.A." Hurley, pioneers of Jefferson County, Kansas. Hurley Family photo

Hurleys, helping Thomas on his hundred and four acres of land. In the census, however, Thomas was named as the father of Barbara's child. Whatever the reason, the newly married couple possibly agreed to raise the boy as their own.

Thomas built a sturdy two-story, four-room log cabin for his growing family. The walls were made of oak and walnut. A large fireplace could burn logs up to four feet long and two feet wide. The roof was covered with oak clapboard shingles, three feet long and two feet wide.

Not new to the area, Mary would tell her children how she'd carried a rifle to school each day, protecting herself and her younger siblings. Northeastern Kansas continued to be perilous. The young family soon discovered a large population of rattlesnakes around their home. On occasion, they also encountered indigenous people living nearby. While the language barrier created uncertainty, these folks were probably more of a concern when Mary was young. Her sons eventually traded ponies with them.

The next decade brought a cup of joy and sorrow to the growing family. George was born in 1871. In the spring, heavy rains flooded streams, washing out bridges and damaging crops. In between the births of Helen and Eli, Barbara's 2-year-old son fell into a well on the farm, and drowned. Some gossiped that Mary may have pushed the boy in, but those close to her said she mourned his death as if he were her own.

Despite all of this, the family forged on. Thomas bought fifty acres of land for seven hundred dollars. Then the grasshoppers returned, destroying everything green within three days. Mary birthed twin girls Mollie and Mary the following winter. When spring arrived, farmers found the nasty calling cards left by last year's grasshoppers: they laid thousands of eggs that hatched and covered everything so thickly that they could be scooped up with a shovel. Then the family suffered yet another blow: baby Mary died.

Thomas replanted his crops, but a severe windstorm and rain damaged the shoots and demolished many buildings. In the summer he replanted corn, which helped him recover. A harsh winter followed, the last straw for hundreds of area citizens who picked up and left the county. It was 1875.

Even as they were burying their fifth child, little four-year-old Helen, Thomas and Mary must have been counting their blessings on one hand and tragedies on the other. All this, after only ten years of marriage. Surely they were beginning to wonder if life would always be such a struggle.

They were not alone, however. Ties between neighbors and families were close and any divisions blurred as they reached out to one another in need. The unspoken code between them was this, as it has always been for rural families: help each other, because it's only a matter of time before you'll need help, too.

Thomas and Mary had their hands full with taking care of the farm and raising half a dozen children, so they hired an emancipated couple named Bob and Tempy Larkins. Thomas and Bob built a second log cabin on the farm for the newcomers to live in. This two-room cabin was about one hundred rods, or more than five hundred yards south of the Hurley cabin.

Tempy helped Mary care for the children. She also cooked, kept the house clean and tended the garden and chickens. Every year or so, she would help bring a new baby into the world: Libbie, young Tom, Will, Jane (who later became known as Jennie), a stillborn infant known only as Baby Hurley, Nora, Nellie, and finally, Ernest.

Never was a hired woman more well-thought of or loved by her young charges than Tempy. When Eli split open his foot between his first and second toes, playing with a hatchet, Tempy took over the job of keeping the wound dressed. "I believe I thought as much of her as I did of Mother," Eli wrote, years later.

The girls hoed in the potato and corn rows and gathered fruits and vegetables. Mary and Tempy sometimes canned as many as four hundred quarts each year. They made their own cider and vinegar, and in a large barrel made kraut and brined down pickles. A huge iron kettle was used to make soap and apple butter. They would store a supply of potatoes and apples in a deep, straw-lined pit to last until next year's harvest.

The children slept four and five at a time, crosswise in two big iron beds, the boys in one and the girls in another. Beginning at 6 a.m., they ate breakfast in shifts. If Mary's calls didn't coax them down to the table, the sound of Thomas' high-top leather boots hitting the stairs would. He'd worn them during the Civil War. They knew their father would be carrying a leather strop at his side. To escape a thrashing, their only escape was to climb out a bedroom window next to the stone chimney, and shimmy down in time to take their places at the table. After the whole clan had eaten, the girls would wash the dishes while the boys did outside chores. All this, before they left for school.

There was plenty of time for exercise and relaxation. On Sunday afternoons in the summer, they rode over to Wolftown and played baseball. Wolftown was a little area that bustled with life on weekends. At the general store, one could buy everything from a hairpin to a buggy. Here, Nate was the catcher and played on a ball team with Tom and Eli. During the winter, they skated and played ice hockey on Stark Lake, east of the Delaware River in Pleasant Valley.

CHAPTER 10

At Huber School

Down the dusty lanes they walked, crossing Rock Creek on a log that spanned the banks when the water was low. Then they trudged up the hill, around a winding lane and along hedge rows to the white schoolhouse. In spring, when the water was high, the Hurley kids could go over to Olive Branch School, since the township line ran through their house.

Twenty or more pairs of shoes clomped into the one-room building every morning, tracking in dirt and mud, softening the unvarnished wood floor. On weekends, Huber School transformed into a gathering place for folks who lived nearby. Saturday nights called for broom busts, or dances. Someone like Harry Kelsch would pull out a fiddle and the grown-ups would dance into the wee hours, the merriment sometimes interrupted by an occasional fistfight or donnybrook. Typically, the men reconciled and threw their arms around each other before the sun came up. On Sunday mornings, Huber schoolhouse transformed into the Free Methodist Church.

The school was three miles by road, from the Hurley homeplace. Nate Isaac's house stood in between. In the winter they walked over fence tops on the frozen, crusted snow. Then they hurried into school to get a prime spot next to a large coal heater in the middle of the room. As the children warmed up, they poked and prodded each other, joking and laughing until Miss Bartel put a stop to their follies with one scornful look over the top of her glasses. She sent the larger, gawky-looking boys to the other side of the room so the smaller ones could sit next to the warmth.

"Class will begin." Miss Bartel silenced the room with a wooden pointer, which she firmly held in her round hands. From the back of the room a giggle pealed out. Three of the larger boys sitting in the back had stuck red-hot candies all over their faces.

"Miss Hurley," the teacher chided, unaware of the boys' antics, "you've been warned before about such outbursts. Since you've no reason to listen, I assume you know the answer to the first math problem."

The slender, dark-haired girl stood up straight in her seat.

"What's the answer?" Miss Bartel demanded, writing figures on the slate with a horrendous screech. Each upstroke of the chalk pierced their eardrums. Jennie winced, covering her ears. She drew a blank. If only she'd listened yesterday. Instead, she watched another girl braid Florence Rickard's hair. It amazed her, how she twisted it around her head.

Just as she was about to give up, just as Miss Bartel was about to give Jennie the awful chore of scrubbing pigeon droppings off the stairs, something touched the back of her hand: a piece of folded-up paper. Stunned that someone was coming to her rescue, Jennie tried to unfold it silently.

"We're waiting," Miss Bartel said impatiently, looking away for just a moment as she tapped her fingernails on the board.

"One hundred... thirty-two!" Jennie choked out.

"What did you say?" Miss Bartel was astonished. How this little girl managed to pull herself out of fixes was incomprehensible.

"One hundred and thirty-two."

She nodded. "That is correct. Next time, pay attention. Your social life can wait until recess."

Jennie caught the eye of her brother Tom. He winked and pointed back at Nate. Jennie didn't know the Isaac boy. Somehow, she wanted to thank him.

By noon, the late winter sun was warmly beating down on the schoolyard. The children braved the cold and took their lunches outside. Each of their little metal pails looked alike. Halfway down the steps, Jennie's brother Will reached over and yanked her hair. Jennie whirled around.

"Who gave you the crib note, Jen? Your new boyfriend? Jennie's got a beau, Jennie's got a beau," Will sang, his friends skipping behind.

Nate sat on a large tree stump on the south side of the schoolhouse with a couple of boys. Their families hadn't weathered the last few years well. He methodically unwrapped two biscuits. Each had a glob of sorghum on top.

Jennie stood behind Nate, her shadow blocking the sun's rays. "Not the best-tasting food, is it? That's all we've had for weeks. I'm getting tired of it, but Mom says our only choice is to go hungry."

Nate looked up at her for a moment, then turned back to his lunch.

"You know what Will and Tom did? They beat the stuffing out of some boys who said, 'All the Hurleys have to eat is biscuits and sorghum.' Well, all they had was bread and honey!"

She turned to Nate's companions. How could she get rid of them long enough to talk to him? "Hey, Will's got two extra jawbreakers. I think he wants to give them away," she said. She laughed, remembering how her brother had hoarded them for weeks. The boys dropped their pails and scurried across the schoolyard.

"Why'd you pass me the note today?" she asked, sitting down next to Nate.

"Who said I did?" he said, not seeming to care.

"You're the only one who could possibly know the answer. You're the only one who listens to Miss Bartel."

"So what if I do? What if I gave you the note?" he asked, irritated.

"Then I'd thank you."

"Oh." He seemed unimpressed, more interested in the biscuit crumbs falling onto his lap.

"I suppose you'll hit me now, or something."

He looked up suddenly. "Why would I do that?"

"That's what my brothers do, when I bother them."

"You're not bothering me."

"Really?"

He shook his head.

"Good, because if you hit me, I'd have to slug you back."

"You fight with your brothers?"

"You bet," she said proudly.

"If I had a sister like you," Nate dared to offer, "I wouldn't be mean."

"Why not?"

"You're pretty."

An awkward silence followed. "How come you never talk to me?" she finally whispered.

"You never talk to me."

"Not so!" she exclaimed.

"Then when?"

"Just the other day you were at the back, near the coat rack, and I said, 'Cold out there, isn't it?'"

"You say that to everyone."

"Well, what do you mean, then?" she asked.

"I just thought... I thought you might like to be friends."

"Give me your hand," she commanded.

"What?"

"Just do it." She shook his hand, grabbed his thumb with hers and said, "There. That's the official Huber School handshake. We're friends now."

"You'll probably get clobbered by Will," he warned.

"Why don't you walk me home today and protect me? Maybe he'll forget about it, and I won't come to school with a black eye tomorrow."

"Even if I could keep him away, that's out of my way. Don't you live a mile or so past my house?"

"You want to be friends, or not?"

Nate chewed his biscuit, thinking for a moment. When he decided to tell her yes, he looked up. She was gone.

CHAPTER 11

The Secret Place

Nate finally caught up to Jennie the following spring. She was halfway home. They stopped in the timber and sat under the boughs of a gnarled oak tree. Jennie leaned against the rough bark, her gingham skirt spread out on the ground around her. Both legs were folded to one side, an arm crooked behind her. Nate noticed it was bent back in a direction that didn't look humanly possible.

"How do you do that?" he asked softly.

"What, this?" she answered, hyperextending her elbow. "I'm double-jointed."

"You mean you have two joints instead of one?"

"No. I don't quite know what it means, other than I can do strange things like this." She pulled her thumb over her wrist and touched the top of her silver bracelet.

"Yuck," he responded, then added quickly, "I'm sorry. I've just never seen anything like that."

"It's okay. I like to do it in front of my brothers. It's the only way I can make them leave me alone."

"Listen to this," he said, folding back the pages of a small, green poetry book. "There was a time when meadow, grove, and stream, the earth and every common sight, to me did seem appareled in celestial light, the glory and the freshness of a dream,'" he read. "What does apparel mean?" he asked, looking up at her brown eyes.

"You know, like clothes."

He nodded and looked down at the page again. Jennie thought Nate made all poetry, no matter how boring, sound wonderful. His accent lilted and tossed the sounds about. Although he was born in Jefferson County, he sometimes hinted at his father's Scottish accent.

"I don't know about celestial," she added apologetically. "Maybe something about the sky. Who wrote that?"

"Fella named Wordsworth. Jennie, you like this place?" He had brought her to the spot where he came to be alone, back in the timber and down a hill, next to the creek. It seemed a world away from the grassy prairie, high above.

"Sure, I guess so."

"It's a secret place. No one but you and I know it's here."

As often as they met in the timber, Jennie snuck into her mother's room and thumbed through prized books. Mary brought several classics with her, on the wagon ride from Ohio to Kansas, and continued adding to her collection. Among them were "The Christian Psalmist," a book of hymns and tunes; "The Greatest Thing in the World" by Henry Drummond, a recently published religious writing; an 1868 version of the New Testament "of Our Lord and Savior Jesus Christ, translated out of the original Greek"; books with pictures of pretty young women on the covers, like Tennyson's "The Princess, A Dream of Fair Women, and Other Poems"; "The Superb Edition of Through a Looking Glass," written by a young writer named Lewis Carroll; a new book written by Robert Louis Stevenson called "Virginibus Puerisque"; "Flora's Dial," which once belonged to Jennie's grandmother and featured a flower and its meaning for each day of the year; and one that had only arrived last week from Chicago called "The Perfect Woman."

This last book intrigued Jennie most, for Mary kept it carefully hidden from the children. However, the young girl happened to see her put it on top of the bedroom armoire. After making sure everyone was downstairs, Jennie pulled the thick book down one day and began to read.

"For maidens—wives—mothers," it began, "a book giving full information on all the mysterious and complex matters pertaining to women." She turned another page to see a drawing of a man and woman standing side by side. They were naked but for a small leaf that covered part of the man's body. Jennie heard footsteps, put the book back, then darted into the room she shared with her younger sisters Nora and Nellie.

"It is, too, a medical book," Mary said forcefully as she and Thomas climbed the stairs. "Look, I'll show you." She reached up on top of the armoire. "That's funny; I thought I put it back here, last night."

Jennie gasped softly.

"Oh, there it is." Mary opened the book. "See? It was written by a doctor."

"A *woman* doctor," Thomas piped up.

"Yes, and she has her M.D. and Ph.D., and graduated from two medical colleges in Chicago. She's also a student at Cook County Hospital, and lectures at the American Health University."

"Women shouldn't have to be doctors," Thomas asserted.

"May I point out that your wife is known for her fine medical skills, here in the county?"

"You're a midwife, Mary. You help neighbors have babies."

"This book has all kinds of information I can use to help them. There are more things I need to learn. Just yesterday I was reading about a way to have a painless childbirth."

Thomas chewed the corner of his mouth. "After all the children you've had, Love, you think that's possible?" He looked down at her widening midriff. "I'd think you could write a book about childbearing, yourself. How much did it cost?"

"One could hardly put a price on it."

"I'll bet the man who sold it to you didn't think so."

"With the payments I've received in the past three months, I've already paid for it."

"Mary, they don't pay you. They give you chickens and eggs, which we really don't need."

"And orange marmalade, which you never turn down, do you?"

He laughed and shook his head.

"I knew you'd see it my way." She gave him a kiss, then cocked her head back. He could almost see her as she was, the first time he laid eyes on her.

CHAPTER12

Two Mothers

Tempy stood at the stove, her slender fingers stained red from cherries. She worked with the confidence and grace of a city chef, cooking them until they were soft at the core. She let them cool before pushing out the cores. Then she dropped them into syrup and cooked them once again. *Plop, plop, plop,* they landed into the thick, steaming bath.

Behind her, the back door flew open. Two brown-headed girls flew in, their loose pigtails flopping.

"Just wait a minute!" Tempy shouted, whirling around and wiping her hands on her apron. "Where you think you're going?"

The ornery pair stopped suddenly and looked up at the ceiling. Nellie held her side and winced. Nora waved her hand back and forth in front of her mouth, as if to force in more air. "Can't… breathe," she whispered dramatically, trying to hide a grin.

"Uh, huh." Tempy's head was cocked to one side. "You're up to no good, I see."

"We aren't. Really!" Nellie choked out.

"Something tells me you were on your way upstairs to see your momma, weren't you?" Aside from cooking and cleaning, Tempy settled arguments, patched wounds and made invisible hurts disappear. Chores could pile up behind her, the more mischief came her way. This week especially, she was attempting to derail any interruptions that robbed Mary of needed rest. Somehow the woman had managed to crack a rib as she leaned down into a barrel.

"You run all the way from the pasture?" Tempy chided. It was as far as Nellie and Nora were allowed to go. Many times she found them sitting on the farthest fencepost. *Always testing their limits,* she thought.

"Cimarron..." Nellie began, unsure how much she should reveal.

"Your Daddy's horse?"

"His favorite mare. We've gotta find Papa!" Nora blurted out.

"He's not here. He's out in the field."

"Will said...."

"I don't care what Will said." Tempy pointed a determined finger at the pair. "Your Momma is upstairs taking a nap. Now, go on back outside. I know those corn rows are just begging to be hoed."

"But Will said that Tom rode Cimmaron."

"He'll have to deal with your Daddy later."

"Tempy," Nellie bravely added, "Tom rode Cimmaron so hard that she was foaming at the mouth, and then he put her back into the barn, wet."

"She's shaking," Nora added.

"Why didn't you say so?" Tempy threw up her hands. "Someone's going to get it! But there's nothing your momma can do about it, so turn right around and head out that door."

"Can we get a drink first?" They stood wide-eyed and paralyzed.

It had been a long day, and these two weren't making it any easier. "Can't you get one from the pump outside?" They still didn't move. "All right," she relented, "but stay close, because as soon as I wash those beans on the table, I'm going to put you out on the front porch so you can snap them for me."

The door slammed, and the girls disappeared.

Tempy shook her head and looked up to heaven. "Thank you, Lord, that Mrs. Hurley is done having babies! One more would be the end of us both."

Upstairs, Mary lay in bed, feeling guilty for leaving Tempy with the canning. She tried to dismiss the fainting spell that had come over her in the morning. The day before, she'd leaned too far down into a pickle barrel, out in the barn. As her short, wide feet left the dirt floor, she heard a loud crack. When she stood up, she felt a sharp pain. The next day she could hardly get out of bed.

Thomas had left before sun-up to work on the new house for Eli and his bride Luie. The men would be back to eat lunch at noon.

Upstairs in her bedroom, Mary looked at her rough, swollen

hands. They had cared for so many children, prepared so many meals. She simply was getting too old to be the mother of a young child. Ernest, the baby, was barely 3, but half of her children now had families of their own.

"How you feeling?" Tempy appeared at Mary's door, offering her a cool washcloth for her forehead.

"About the same," she answered flatly.

"Let's see those ribs," Tempy insisted.

"They're fine. Nothing a little rest won't take care of. I just need to lay here a few more minutes, and then I'll come downstairs and help." Mary tried in vain to sit up on the edge of the bed.

Tempy laid her back down, gently. "Mrs. Hurley, we're going to have to bind those ribs now, and you're going to help me do it." When Mary loosened her blouse, Tempy tried to hide her astonishment, seeing how large the woman had become. Her girth had increased with each child. *Round as the barrel she fell into,* Tempy thought. *A wonder she didn't get stuck!*

"Oh my goodness," Mary said weakly, looking down at Tempy's apron.

"What's wrong?" she asked, thinking she had put too much pressure on her ribs. "Those must be good and cracked, for sure."

Mary's face turned white. "Is that my..." she began to ask, staring down at Tempy's red-stained apron.

She followed Mary's eyes. "Oh, good heavens," she said, covering her mouth, then laughing and patting the woman's arm to comfort her. "That's not your blood, that's cherry juice!"

Mary blinked, looking closer to make sure, then laughed until the pain made her stop. "What's been going on, downstairs?"

"Those two little ones just came barreling through. Now, why did I tell you that? You just need to let me take care of everything."

"What are they up to?"

"Well, they came running into the house, going on about one of the boys and Mr. Hurley's horse."

A voice bellowed downstairs. "Who's been riding Cimmaron?" The ranting increased, changing from English to Gaelic, and everything in between. Thomas' boot soles hit the front porch where Will sat deep in thought, swinging his legs back and forth, whittling on a piece of pine.

"I want to know, and I want to know now!" Thomas bellowed. "Who's been riding my horse?" He snatched the wood out of Will's hand and threw it to the ground. "Pay attention, boy!" Thomas lifted his chin so his eyes met his father's. "Someone's been riding Cimarron. I gave no one permission to ride her. Who would be foolish to do such a thing?"

"Don't know, sir."

"Do you know what I'll do, when I find them?"

"Tom did it!" he blurted out.

"Tom?"

"Yes, Tom!"

"How do you know?"

"Told me so!"

"Where is he?"

"In the barn, I think. Dad," he added quickly, "don't tell him I told you."

"When I get through with that boy, he won't be able to sit for a week." Thomas stormed into the house, taking two stairs at a time. "Where's my shillelagh?" he called to the stunned women.

"Hanging behind the door," Mary responded quickly, looking worried. The handle was made from the branch of a blackthorn tree, three inches across—just the right size to put into a man's hand. Extending out from this was another knobby branch as big around as Thomas' thumb, and more than a foot long. It was a brutal and powerful weapon in the hands of someone who knew how to use it. Most of the time, its sheer presence was enough to keep everyone in line.

Mary shuddered as Thomas grabbed the weapon and bounded down the stairs. "How is it that every time he disciplines someone, it hurts me more?" she wondered.

CHAPTER 13

Looking Ahead

"Don't dog-ear the pages, don't leave it outside, and most importantly, bring it back tomorrow or I'll catch thunder." Jennie reached into her dress pocket and pulled out a new poetry book for Nate to read.

"I know, I know," he replied, accustomed to her warnings. On their way to the special place in the timber, Jennie's dog rubbed his cold, wet nose against her hand. She reached down to pat Shep on the head to let him know he was welcome to come along.

"Someday," Nate vowed, "I'll memorize all your favorite poems, and then I won't need to borrow your mother's books." The small, red volume fit neatly in the palm of his hand.

"Really Nate, it's all right," she said. "I know you love to read. Besides, since Ernest was born, Momma hasn't had much time to look at them. If she could see you like this, I'm sure she'd be glad to loan them to you." She was sneaking the books out of the house—no small accomplishment, considering the number of people roaming about. Having a secret excited Jennie; doing it to please a boy made it more enjoyable.

"Psst. Over here," a voice whispered from inside the bushes.

"Who's there?" Jennie called out.

"Tom," the voice answered.

"What are you doing in there?"

"Trying to find Will. Have you seen him?"

"No, why?"

There was a pause. Tom emerged from the brush, bent over and rubbing his backside.

"What happened?" Jennie said, laughing. Nate was beginning to chuckle, too.

"I took a beating for Will. He told Dad that I was the one who rode Cimarron."

"Did you do it?" Jennie asked.

"No, and when I find him, he's gonna get it twice as hard as I did!" Tom slowly backed away.

"Those two," Jennie laughed. "They're always trying to get each other."

"Better them, than you," Nate remarked.

"They don't pick on me anymore. Dad made them stop. Said it wasn't gentlemanly to get beat up by a girl."

They both laughed. Nate looked down at the book. "Pa says I shouldn't waste my time with things that aren't farming."

"Is that why you don't go to church?"

"Suppose so." He felt left out on Sundays. The entire Hurley clan, minus Thomas, was away from the house all morning. Sometimes Nate made a couple of trips down the hill to see if they'd returned. They all looked so nice, dressed in their finest clothing. "What's it like?" he asked.

"Some hymn singing, some Bible reading, and some prayers. The grownups spend all this time talking, afterward! We used to go to the Catholic Church until Daddy got mad at the priest." She was referring to the day that the priest came knocking on their door for tithe money. Apparently, he'd done this one too many times. Exasperated, Thomas asked the white-collared clergyman, "How do you expect me to keep giving to the church when I have so many mouths to feed?"

With some empathy the priest replied, "Thomas, giving to the Lord is a way of showing your devotion. If you give to the Lord first and use the rest to take care of your family, you might have more abundance in your life."

Thomas stood there a moment, trying to understand something that called for more faith than he possessed. The unintended message he received was that he wasn't a good provider. "Father, don't ever darken me door again," he said bluntly. Turning to his family, he pointed at them and said, "And don't any of you ever darken the door of a Catholic church, either!"

After some time passed, Mary convinced Thomas to drive her and the younger children to Huber School on Sundays. He would only attend when someone was baptized or married. However, his belief in Jesus Christ and the Resurrection never wavered. "Even if you cannot accept all of its assertions as fact," the simple Irishman said, "you have nothing to lose, and everything to gain. If it's true, you will have gained eternity; if it's not, you will have lived a better life." His children remembered this for the rest of their lives.

"Momma's getting baptized again, next Sunday in Rock Creek," Jennie told Nate one day. "That is, assuming her ribs heal up. Want to come?"

"Don't think I'd fit in," Nate said.

"We'll be outside. It won't be like a regular church service." She knew he wouldn't be easily convinced. "Nate Isaac, are you scared of church people?"

"No."

"They won't hold you down and baptize you against your will, for goodness' sake!"

"What's so great about it, anyway?"

"The priest used to say it's God's way of naming and claiming us as His own. Even as babies. And that we get the Holy Spirit when it happens. But this new pastor says Momma needs to be baptized again, if she wants to join his church." He really had no idea what she was talking about. "Besides, I just love all that hymn singing. And it makes Momma hum and smile for days."

"Do your brothers go?"

"Sometimes. It's like a big family there, Nate. People who care about you, like having more brothers and sisters."

"Can you talk in church?"

"Only when a grownup asks you a question, and then you're supposed to whisper."

"Why?"

"Out of respect. You also shouldn't run or yell when you're there. Like walking on the tips of your toes when your Dad is in a bad mood."

"Does God get angry at us?"

"I suppose, when we do things He doesn't want us to."

"How do we know what that is?"

"By reading the Bible. Nate, just come to church with me sometime, and you'll see."

He lay back in the grass. "You know, I don't read with anyone but you."

"That's because I'm the only one who brings you books."

Nate rose up on his elbows. "Cordy Logan gave me a book of songs, only they were dumb. Just words to music I'd never heard."

"Want to hear a secret?" she asked. "Someday I'm going to leave this place and become famous."

"How?"

"Maybe I'll become a famous opera singer. Maybe someday, when I move to Kansas City."

He looked at her blankly. "Can you sing?"

"Of course. Daddy's going to buy me a piano, if the wheat crop is good."

"We could have a drought, or it could hail. What's so exciting about Kansas City?"

"There's a lot going on there! Art, music, theatre. Maybe one day you can come see. My piano teacher says I should start taking voice lessons. Nate, what are you going do when you grow up?"

"Reckon I'll just stay right here, Jennie, and be a farmer."

"Aren't you itching to get out of here?"

"Not really. If I left, it'd be for just a short while to earn some money and buy some land."

"You'd be a good farmer, Nate, but you could do something more. You're smart. You've always been able to out-figure me in math." She rolled onto her stomach and picked a ladybug out of his hair. "First chance I get, I'll leave this place. I think I belong in the city."

Nate laughed. "Jennie, you're no different than anyone else."

"I am different, and I think I should have finer things in life. Maybe I'll marry someone rich, and get a diamond ring as big around as the end of my finger." She showed him how big it was.

He looked at her pretty white hands. "Maybe I could buy you one, someday. If I made enough money farming."

"Why don't you come with me and wear some fancy clothes? You could work in a big building and never get dirty. Just look at all those callouses on your hands!"

"I don't think that kind of life is for me."

"Aren't you tired of working so hard?"

"Work isn't bad. Makes you strong. Being lazy makes a body weak."

"I work hard."

He laughed.

"I do! Cleaning the house, helping Tempy cook, beating the rugs and hanging out the laundry."

"Try shucking a wagon full of corn, or herding cattle, or leading a team through the mud. Besides, what'll you do in the city?"

"Probably get my teaching certificate. Find someone to write me a letter of recommendation so I can work in the city. You'll see; I'll get there." She paused. "Will you miss me when I'm gone?"

"Of course," he replied sadly.

"We'll always be connected to each other, and this place," she said.

He reached down and pulled a handful of dogtooth violets from the ground, and gave them to her.

She grabbed him by the neck and kissed him. It was May, and the leaves were just beginning to unfold.

CHAPTER 14

The Injustice of It All

Nate never would've guessed, but his opinion of Jennie changed in just one day. It happened when he saw her react to a new student at Huber School. Instead of welcoming her, Jennie wanted nothing to do with the girl. She could've been interested and politely asked about her hometown—Kansas City—but instead, Jennie couldn't seem to get far enough away.

The boys, she said, hung around the new girl like deer to a salt block. "Can we help you with your homework?" they offered. They fought over who would carry her books home. This constant attention annoyed Jennie. She sat and watched from afar, seething.

She remembered their teacher, Miss Bartel, cupping her hands on Vera's shoulders and presenting their new classmate that day like a show-and-tell doll. Jennie imagined this was likely the beginning of many painful days.

"Class, this is Vera Samuelson, and she'll be attending Huber School until spring." Miss Bartel looked down at the girl's sweet face. "She's staying in Fairview Township with her grandparents. Everyone, please make Vera feel welcome."

Well, this won't do, Jennie thought. *Doesn't she know that I'm supposed to be the most popular girl in school? Why doesn't someone tell her that her hairstyle is out of fashion?*

"Vera, why don't you sit beside Jennie?" she heard the teacher say. "I'm sure you two will get along fine."

"Oh, wonderful," Jennie said aloud to the girl sitting in front of her, rolling her eyes. Miss Bartel told her she also had to share her books and inkwell. Didn't she already have to share everything at home? To make matters worse, Vera decided to tag along after Jennie. Unfortunately, the more hateful Jennie became, the more Vera clung to her.

As others offered help, Vera gradually drifted from Jennie. This was fine with her, but she was upset that the kids were putting Vera on a pedestal. During recess one day, Jennie stayed inside and drew on the slate the ugliest picture she could imagine. Underneath it she wrote, "This is Vera." When the children came in, the teacher asked who'd done such a thing. Of course, Jennie didn't own up to it. She started counting the days until April came, and Vera was gone.

As Jennie put on her coat to leave one afternoon, she was once again confronted by a swarm of boys following Vera. "We get together every Sunday down at Stark Lake to go skating," one of them explained.

"Yes, and we want to make sure you come this weekend," another added.

"I'd like to, but I'm quite unprepared," Vera said in a crisp city style. "You see, I didn't bring any skates with me."

"No problem. We'll find a pair for you," a quick-thinking young man offered. Others nodded in agreement.

"I don't get it! What does she have that I don't?" Jennie asked, not caring who heard. Then letting out a heavy sigh, she threw up her hands.

"I don't know," Tom said, grinning, "but she sure is cute!"

Jennie swung her schoolbooks, hitting him in the gut. "Why do you talk so funny?" she called out to Vera.

Scrapping was the last thing Vera wanted, so she did her best to keep conversation light. "What do you mean?"

"You must think you're better than all of us. You talk so uppity."

"This is how everyone in Kansas City speaks. It's not odd, there. I suppose people from Kansas City might think you sound odd."

Kansas City! Jennie thought. How dare Vera imply that Jennie wouldn't fit in. Besides, if Vera really was from Kansas City, that was the last place Jennie wanted to go. She'd rather move to St. Louis or Chicago. She could be a famous singer anywhere.

The air was calm, the sky clear—perfect for skating. Vera showed up in a red coat with a fur collar. It was unlike anything the kids at Huber School wore. Maybe it was fashionable in the city, but Jennie decided she'd rather be cold than to wear something so bright and obnoxious.

Like hawks swooping down to grab a fish, several boys jumped through the snow to reach Vera. They pointed her to a log sitting beside the bank. Once she sat down, they helped her try on all sizes of skates. One boy sat at her feet until he was convinced she had the right pair.

Just like a silly fairytale princess, Jennie thought, sarcastically. Nate must have sensed what she was thinking, because he came up behind her and grabbed her arm.

"Come on. Let's skate."

"Just look at her," Jennie hissed. The boys were still jockeying for position so they could help Vera stand up on her skates and walk over to the edge of the ice. "They never sat in the snow for me," Jennie said wistfully.

"Oh Jennie, this isn't about you. It's just that someone new is here," Nate explained. "That's the only reason she's got their attention."

Vera and her entourage skated past. "Tell us more about the city," the boys pleaded. "How big is it?"

"Have you seen one of those horseless carriages?" they bombarded. "Do they really have telephones?"

"Yes, thanks to the Home and Bell telephone companies. There are so many wonderful things that I cannot begin to tell you everything. Many people ride a streetcar to work but a few have horseless carriages. I rode in one last summer. It was a prototype."

"A what?"

"You know, an original."

"Wow," the boys chimed together.

"And I've personally seen the backside of a horse," Jennie mimicked from the other side of the lake. "In fact...."

"Jennie," Nate warned.

"I'm looking at one, right now!" She pointed at Vera, who began to turn the color of her coat. For a moment, not a sound was heard across the ice.

Jennie lifted the back of her hand to her forehead. "Save me from this cold, cruel world," she mocked.

Nate flashed a disapproving look, then hopped off the ice to leave Jennie alone in the mess she'd created. Undaunted, she skated up to a circle of girls who'd stopped to watch the mounting scene. "Can you believe her?"

"I think Kansas City must be the best place in the whole world!" Nate yelled, trying to create a distraction.

"I don't know about you," Jennie whispered to the girls, "but I've had about all I can take of our visitor. I think it's time we teach her a lesson."

"You're right, Nate," Vera called out. "In fact, a lot of people say it's the best place to raise a family."

"Why on earth is that?" Jennie pushed.

"There's just no substitute for good breeding," Vera answered, looking Nate's way, trying to avoid Jennie's eyes.

"Isn't that how farm animals are made?" Jennie yelled from across the ice. "How would you know anything about that?" Her small group of supporters laughed.

"You'd know more about that, than I do," Vera answered flippantly.

Jennie bit down on her lip. "So we're not good enough for you."

"I didn't say that," Vera started to explain.

"Why don't you go back to Kansas City and leave us stupid farm kids alone?"

Stunned young skaters looked back and forth between the two girls to see what would happen next. They could feel it in their bones; an incident was about to happen that would become legendary. Everyone would claim they were there on that fateful day.

"I never meant to say that you were less important than me," Vera said softly, tears welling up in her eyes. "Or not as smart."

Jennie skated across the lake and stopped a few feet in front of her. "You know what? I think I'm better than you, because you came from Kansas City and ended up here. I was born here, and I'll end up in Kansas City one day, or someplace even better."

"I don't know why you're so upset," Vera said honestly. "I was just trying to answer their questions."

"I think it's time you realized a few things. First, Kansas City isn't the best place in the world. Second, you're not the only girl in our school. And third, your behavior is quite inappropriate."

"Jennie!" Nate hissed.

In an effort to silence him, Jennie held out her arm. "No. I'm not through. In fact, I'm just beginning. Vera Samuelson, what do you have that we don't?"

Tears spilled from Vera's eyes.

"We're waiting for an answer. You do have one, don't you?"

Vera looked down. "I'm sorry," she said softly, shaking her head.

"C'mon, Jen. You can't be serious," her brother Tom interjected. Normally, he took the side of his family, but she had gone too far.

"I just want to hear what she really thinks, so we can get on with our skating. But maybe Vera wants to drag this on until spring, when the ice melts."

"We have culture," Vera said bravely, shaking.

"Culture?"

"Yes. Art museums and music theatres."

"Well, lah-di-dah."

"My mother says it's the only thing that separates people from animals."

Jennie looked at Vera hard, trying to guess why she would say such a dumb thing. So did the rest of the onlookers. "Could you please say that again? I want to make sure everyone heard."

"Maybe that came out wrong."

"I'm guessing so. She thinks we're animals," Jennie said to the crowd. "Now the truth comes out!"

"Jennie, you're making way too much of this," Will said. He turned to Vera. "She gets like this sometimes. Just don't say anything more."

"Will, butt out. This is between her and I now."

"Her and me," Vera corrected, unable to stop herself.

"What?" Jennie bellowed.

"What did I do to make you so mad? You've been hateful ever since I came here."

"Have not," Jennie said defiantly.

"Yes, you have," Vera said. The crowd nodded in agreement.

"I have an idea. Let's settle this, once and for all. You do know how to skate, right?"

"Yes. Every winter, on Troost Lake."

"Let's see how you skate against a wild animal, then."

The onlookers formed a circle around the lake edge, cheering and clapping as the two girls started to race. They lined up together, at one end of the lake. One boy pulled off his scarf and waved it, starting them. Jennie took the early lead. "First one to fall, loses," she yelled at Vera, who was already behind her. "Winner gets a full apology in front of the whole class."

Vera threw her weight into it, edging closer, until Jennie let an elbow fly. Vera winced, but became more determined.

Jennie had no way of knowing that this was just another case of someone pushing Vera too far. She had come to Huber School because she'd been shipped off to her grandparents while her parents worked out the terms of their impending divorce. In time, they would decide who should have custody of her. Neither seemed especially interested because it interfered with their social lives. Vera overheard them arguing one night, about who would pay the nanny to watch her.

No, being nice just didn't pay off, Vera reasoned. So she let Jennie Hurley have a taste of all the sorrow and anger she'd crammed down inside, these past few months. She reached out to grab Jennie's shoulder but got a handful of brown hair, instead. Jennie let out a frightening scream. *Was she hurt,* the spectators wondered, *or mad with rage?*

The skating stopped. Both girls came together, hitting each other, their arms flying overhead in slapping motions that caused little harm. No punches were thrown. No one had ever seen such a thing. It was how little girls fought, when tempers flared.

CHAPTER 15

Away from Home

Vera left when springtime came, but things were never quite the same. Jennie was no longer the sweet, innocent girl Nate had grown fond of. He was still drawn to her, but wiser. Now he knew she could lash out whenever she felt threatened. For a time, even he was careful to weigh his words and tried to make her feel important.

Circumstances separated them more. Nate walked down the road to work for the Hubers, one day. There, he received fifteen dollars a month, along with room and board. Jennie rode over to Crescent Grove to take both halves of her teacher's diploma test. When she received the news she'd passed, her father drove her to sister Maggie's house in Meriden. Jennie took a teaching position there, and helped her keep the two-story house clean. Maggie's husband Ben Bowlby was much older, only seven years younger than Thomas. Once, he was a drummer boy in the Civil War. Now he served as city commissioner and also was Meriden's bank president.

The Bowlby house was fancier than the new farmhouse Thomas was building for Eli and Luie. Maggie's house was located just outside Meriden's city limits, two blocks west of Palmberg and Wyandotte streets. Spindle railings extended along the front porch and sides. The trim was painted dark to match the black wrought iron fence that girded the property. Three statuesque maples stood close to the road. A landscaper pruned large evergreens into balls, making them appear as if they'd been stacked on a rod.

Inside, the walls were covered with lithographs and paintings in heavily ornate frames. Carpets covered most of the hardwood floors. The front entrance boasted a small library of books. Each glass-front bookshelf opened from the bottom. A large portrait of Ben stood on an easel. In the parlor, exquisite lace curtains hung from ceiling to floor. Tasseled footstools sat in front of the tapestry upholstered furniture. A rich, cherry clock rang out warmly on the quarter hour.

Jennie thought Maggie had done quite well for herself. *Surely I belong among all this finery,* she thought as she helped Maggie pour tea from a large silver urn for the Ladies' Aid Society. Jennie hoped her sister's friends and new teaching position would help her climb the social ladder and become more well known, so that she could escape this rural setting.

The rest of the Hurley family spread out from the farm. Mollie married the moustachioed Dan Pepper, a farmer in Fairview and Rock Creek townships. Libbie worked as a servant for the Goepferts in Kentucky Township. Andy lived with Mollie and Dan, and helped with farmwork. Will worked over in Dickinson County.

After a rabbit hunt, near the Hurley homeplace: Tom Hurley (son of T.A.), Ernest Hurley and Dan Pepper (Mollie Hurley's husband). Hurley Family photo

George ventured out to Colorado to try his hand at mining. That left Tom, Nora, Nellie and Ernest at home.

Dan came to the Hurley farm with Mollie at least once a week to go hunting with the family. Sometimes the men were so successful that young Ernest, wearing an oversized hunting jacket, had to drop some of the rabbits and squirrels along the road as the hunting party walked ahead. Sometimes his nephew Lester, Libbie's son who was eight years younger, would tag along and do the same.

Thomas helped Bob and Tempy move to Topeka. Their old cabin became storage for fanning mill seeds like millet, wheat, buckwheat, oats and flax. It also housed a one-horse cultivator, a walking plow and a couple of barrels. Thomas also stored his tobacco there. All the boys except Ernest tried chewing or smoking it.

Eli and Luie lived in the main cabin for several months until the new house on the north forty acres was finished. Mary and Luie sewed enough rags to lay twenty-eight yards of carpet in the front room. They also made three bed comforts, and canned fruits and butters. For some reason, they moved the grape butter to the upstairs floor. As the weather got warmer, the two-quart jars blew up, making a big blue spot that leaked through the floor and down through the ceiling.

Originally, there were just two rooms on the main floor. Eli and Luie purchased all new furniture and slept upstairs in the summertime. Although it was unfinished, they could open the windows on each side and let in a cool breeze.

Their first baby Theodore was born at the new house. Luie was too exhausted and anemic to take care of the boy and feed him properly in his first few days. The child died soon after. Maggie and Belle Becker, a neighbor, stayed at the house with Luie. They buried the infant on the coldest, harshest day that Luie could remember.

"To lay a baby away, out in that storm, was the hardest thing I think any mother ever done," Luie later wrote. It nearly broke her heart. "After many years, I came to see that it was for the best, but I never forgot the way he looked into my eyes just as he died."

Luie and Eli's next child, Lucile, was also born in the new house. She arrived at 2 a.m. The doctor, Belle and Mary (who Luie called "Mother Hurley") were there to make sure the baby thrived. Belle washed and dressed Lucile, wrapped her in a blanket, and laid her in bed next to Luie. "Look at her!" Belle said. "She's looking all around, just like a two-month-old would."

The bright-eyed infant hardly cried, and finally went to sleep. "Are you sure she's all right?" Luie kept asking that morning.

"Yes, yes," Belle assured, placing a breakfast plate in front of Luie. "I'll stay until the afternoon, if you like."

"She's nursing all right," Mary observed. "My, isn't she beautiful?"

"The most beautiful child I think I've ever seen," Belle chimed in.

Luie and little Lucile became inseparable. When Luie became pregnant again, she was so tired that she could hardly get her chores done. Lucile, not quite 3, tried to help her mother in her own way. One day, she went out to the coop to gather eggs. When she tried to pull an old setting hen off her nest, the hen pecked Lucile's hands until they bled.

The same year, Luie tied up a hen and placed her with a brood of chicks next to the house. Lucile thought one of the chicks was wandering off too far, so she picked it up. As the little girl stooped over to talk to the chick, the old mother hen clucked loudly. Lucile was so surprised that she tumbled over. The hen perceived this sudden move as a threat and flopped all over Lucile, pecking at her hands and face. After those two painful mishaps, Lucile didn't want anything to do with chickens again.

On Halloween, Luie went into labor. Mary and Matt Self's wife were there to help. When they handed Eli his new daughter, all he could say to his wife was, "I told you I wanted a boy."

"Hold your horses," Mary said, attending the birth. "Maybe this next one is a boy."

Next one? Eli thought. Months earlier, Luie told him she thought she was carrying twins, but he didn't believe her. After all, she hadn't seen a doctor to confirm it. Now, Dr. Work was here with them, arriving just in time to deliver that second baby. Just like Eli's mother guessed, it was a boy. They named the newborns Maude and Claude.

Luie always dreamed about her babies, and claimed she saw them before she knew she was pregnant. That's why she thought she was having twins. She dreamed that two babies were sitting in the big, old rocking chair in the kitchen. One baby was very light, with blue eyes. The other was dark and smaller. Strangely enough, each baby turned out exactly as they appeared in her dream. They even posed the two in similar fashion for their first photograph.

When Maude and Claude were two weeks old, Eli decided to have a sale and move to Topeka. "I'm tired of farming," he announced one evening as Luie was nursing the babies. He was working hard, farming fifty acres of his father's land. Truth was, he was more tired of the growing tension in his family. Some of his siblings thought it wasn't right that the young couple lived in a house nicer than their parents'.

"Well, you know what? I'm tired of washing all of these baby clothes, and hanging them up around the stove to dry," Luie echoed. "Besides, Claude can't keep anything down."

"Why not?"

"The doctor says I've been poisoning him with my milk. Just haven't been able to get enough sleep."

"I thought he was supposed to get better when you put Maude on that cow's milk formula."

"Guess that hasn't worked. So tell me, how am I supposed to get any rest if I've got to pack for a move?"

"We'll just sell everything, except what we absolutely need."

With five people in the house, there was always a full tub of washing for the laundry. Before long, they all got sick from the damp air. Luie tended to Claude, who was terribly ill. That left little Lucile with no one to care for her.

The family was alone for three weeks until help arrived. By that time, Claude had pneumonia. The doctor came to check on him, and found he had a fever of 107 degrees. Claude probably wouldn't live, he told them.

Soon the Hurley family came to help. Mrs. Darling, an old neighbor, spent the night. On his way home, the doctor stopped at the Beckers and told Belle what was going on. Luie would not trust anyone but Belle to give Claude's medicine correctly, so her husband took her to stay with them a few days.

The doctor gave Belle a capsule and told her to give it to Luie so she could sleep. Luie undressed for the first time in three weeks, and went to bed. With Maude by her side, she slept soundly through the night. Eli went upstairs to sleep, just as he had since the twins were born. Lucile slept in Luie's room in a baby bed loaned from a neighbor.

Every night after that, Luie got up to feed the babies every two hours. She noticed that Lucile would open her eyes each time and sit up in bed. "No wonder Lucile grew up older than her years," Luie later commented. "Seems she was always looking after babies or children."

Claude struggled but made it through the tough ordeal. When he recovered, Eli's family affirmed what he and Luie had been thinking: they thought the couple should move out of the house so Mary and Thomas could live there. Dr. Work advised Eli to move his family to Meriden, where he could keep an eye on the twins.

Maggie found a nearby house for sale, and the family moved there in April. She helped Eli get a job on the railroad, where he worked for a section gang. He dug ditches three days a week and found more work at Harry Ploughe's farm. The only time he went home was between Saturday night and Monday morning.

Soon after, Maggie took over. She had no children of her own but started telling Luie how to take care of the three little ones. Maggie fed Claude the wrong kind of food, and it wasn't long before he developed rickets and became deathly ill again. Luie tried desperately to get word to Eli at the Ploughe farm.

"Why didn't you try to reach me?" he later asked Luie.

"I did. I sent word with everyone who might be close by."

"Thank goodness Maggie called. She said you haven't been taking care of Claude." Eli bent over the boy to feel his forehead.

Luie laughed angrily. "She's the one who's been going against the doctor's orders and giving him things he shouldn't eat. She won't let me near him, Eli. She's over here all the time."

"Maggie wants to take Claude and raise him herself." Luie couldn't believe what she was hearing. Eli looked up at her. "She loves him, and they've got the money to raise him properly."

"You can't be serious, Eli. Give away our child? How could you even think of it?" She began to sob.

"We've got the other children to care for. Besides, Maggie doesn't have any of her own."

"I didn't carry my kids so she could have her pick! If Maggie wanted children, she should've married a younger man."

"Luie," he scolded.

"Don't you see? Maggie's the reason Claude is this way. If she'd leave us alone, we'd be fine."

"We also wouldn't have any money for groceries."

"I know. We'll get by. Anything would be better—anywhere would be better—as long as we're far from Maggie. You know I love your family, Eli, but I also love this family—*our* family—and I don't want anything to happen to us. I'd rather die."

He sat down beside her. "Remember when we used to go to the magic lantern picture show?" he said wistfully. "We had so much fun."

"Yes. We used to go dancing, too."

"Let's not forget about us, what used to be. I know things were easier before the kids, before I had to be gone so much. But one thing hasn't changed; I still love you with my whole heart. And I'm determined that nothing will ever come between us, Luie."

The next day, Eli had a talk with Maggie. He let her know that they'd be keeping Claude. No sooner had he left for work then Maggie stomped over to the house and had a few words with Luie.

"I will turn him away from you, if it's the last thing I do," Maggie said coldly, then turned on her heels and left.

When Eli got back and saw how distressed Luie was again, he made plans to move his family fifteen miles west, to Hoyt.

CHAPTER 16

Letters from Teacher

Dear Nate,

I am teaching 2nd primary again, here in Meriden. Last year, I had forty pupils; this year, I have twenty-seven. Some of the children are so unruly I wonder what our world is coming to. We never would have been so disrespectful. One boy always lies down on the seat and sticks his feet out the window. I've told him a dozen times not to, so when he did it again yesterday, I lost my patience and broke a book over his head. I know that sounds awful, but he really wasn't hurt badly. The principal called me in to say the boy's parents were taking him out of school for a week. I say, good riddance.

I suppose you heard Eli and Luie left the farm. Maggie is sad. She'll miss the children but I know it's for the best. Mother is so glad to be able to live in her new house.

—Jennie

In the next few years, the house was added on to, making five rooms downstairs. Sunlight flooded the parlor first thing in the morning. Next to this was the dining room, where the grandchildren grabbed Thomas' pocket watch from the table and hid it. They did this to see him "get his Irish up," which manifested in a mix of Gaelic and English cursing that no one could understand. The kitchen was on the southwest corner and emptied onto a large screened-in back porch, also directly behind the dining room. The stairs led up to at least four bedrooms.

The children watched for times when Thomas would wind the weight clock on the fireplace mantel. Sometimes they'd see him pull out a little bag of gold dust, a reminder of his Colorado mining days. This also was an insurance policy in case times got tough. However, Thomas was so sentimental about his younger adventurous life that he never cashed it in.

Dear Nate,

Can you believe I'm here in McLouth, almost twenty miles from home? I find this very exciting. I'm planning to give up my long underwear this winter, since no one's here to tell me otherwise. I'm living with the Reynolds family. They're nice folks. Maybe I'll keep moving east and get to Kansas City someday. Wouldn't Vera's jaw drop if I showed up on her doorstep?

You'll never guess what happened the other day. A man who lost his wife and has a bunch of children to raise cornered me in the doorway of the schoolhouse at the end of the day. His intentions weren't innocent. He wouldn't let me pass, and was beginning to smother me. I told him to go ahead and do what he planned, because I'd just go to the newspaper office and make sure the whole thing was in next week's paper. So far, he's left me alone.

See you at Thanksgiving,

Jennie

Despite their constant bickering and differences of opinions, the Hurley clan returned to the farm for large gatherings. The family grew exponentially with each marriage and birth. Mary was especially thankful for her large, new house on Sundays and holidays, since the cabin never could have held all those bodies.

Mary was set on having things just right. She instructed the girls and young women how to starch and iron the freshly laundered tablecloths and napkins. Then the silver would be polished. She worked days ahead to prepare huge gobblers and ganders, and pumpkin pies. Her spiced fruit and pickles added to the table. Only Mary's best china and ceramic bowls, gifts from her sons, were fit for such occasions.

After dinner, when the dishes were carefully washed and put away, the grown-ups gathered in the parlor to sing hymns and popular songs. Jennie usually accompanied them on her new piano. They engaged in lively conversation while the children played outside, underneath the big maple tree.

Dear Nate,

Well, you won't believe this, but I just received word that my application is being considered by the Kansas City school district! If I'm accepted, I'd like to take some private voice lessons, as you know I've always dreamed. Can you believe it's finally going to happen? I'm so excited that I'll soon be moving out of Jefferson County. Oskaloosa is a nice place to teach, but I must keep moving forward.

I know that boys will be boys, but the ones around here are especially rowdy. I bought a horse from two of my older pupils. Every time I ate lunch in my wagon, and set the clock to ring so I could wake up from a nap and go back to the schoolhouse, the horse would take off like it had been shot in the backside. It nearly killed me before the boys told me it was a racehorse, trained to run when it heard a bell. I sold it back to them and gave them a good tongue lashing.

Remember the boy I whacked on the side of the head in Meriden? He drove over last week to see if I wanted to go for a ride. I obliged, but had to keep reminding him to keep his hands to himself. Good thing he listened. He's much bigger. Not sure I could've fended him off.

Bound for Kansas City,
Jennie

Jennie Hurley, or Genevieve, as a teenager. Hurley Family photo

Thomas Andrew Hurley home, 5 mi. SE of Meriden, Kan. From left: Faye Baker Self, Genevieve Pepper, Mollie Hurley Pepper, T.A. Hurley and Ernest Hurley.

Tom Hurley (left) with a cinnamon bear strapped to a sled. He shot it with a friend at Crystal Peak, NE of Steamboat Springs, Colo. Taken in front of the Steamboat Creamery. Hurley Family photo

T.A. Hurley with his son Tom, in Talmage, Kan. Hurley Family photo

Maggie Hurley Bowlby, eldest daughter in the Hurley family. Hurley Family photo

Alonzo “Lon” Myers, soon after he was engaged to Jennie Hurley. Charles Myers Collection. Used with permission.

Helen “Holly” Cook, Ernest Hurley’s new bride. Gene Cook Collection. Used with permission.

A family gathering at the Hurley home. Back row, left to right: Ernest Hurley, Thomas Andrew Hurley, unknown man, Mary Hurley (apron), unknown woman and baby, Luie Hurley, unknown girl, Dan Pepper, Jennie Hurley, Eli Hurley and Nellie Hurley. Lady in front of Jennie: Mollie Hurley Pepper. Children in front, left to right: Lucile Hurley (next to Mary Hurley), Elsie Pepper, unknown girl, Lawrence Pepper, Claude Hurley and Maude Hurley. Ca. 1908. Hurley Family photo

Tom, Genevieve/Jennie, Ernest, Nellie and George Hurley. Hurley Family photo

CHAPTER 17

A Reunion

Jennie was home for summer less than a day when Nate appeared at the door of the Hurley house. "Well hello, Nathan Isaac." She greeted him with a kiss on the cheek and a hug around his neck. He was stunned by this sudden affection.

"Come on, Shep," she called, slapping her leg as he walked with them, down the boardwalk. "Are the dogtooth violets still in bloom?" she asked Nate.

"Haven't been out in the timber this week. Been busy cutting wheat."

"Oh yes," she said. "You know, once you've been away from home, you lose track of what's going on. I did notice it looked like a nice crop."

"Best in years," he added. "Don't know where they're going to put it all."

"Nate, let's talk about something else. Did you know that I'm moving to Kansas City this fall?"

"Are you sure?"

"Yes!" she squeaked, putting her hand over her mouth. "Oh Nate, it's a dream come true. I have to keep pinching myself." She reached for an envelope in her apron pocket and handed it to him. "This came yesterday."

He pulled out a formal-looking piece of paper and scanned the page. "I'm happy for you, Jen," he said, looking up with a forced smile.

"What's wrong? You don't look like it."

"I am."

"This shouldn't come as a surprise."

"You've been gone so long, and now that you're back, you're already planning to leave again. What if you don't come back this time?"

"I promise to. Why don't you write back?"

"Been busy working. But I think of you."

"Did you get another girlfriend?" she teased. "Have you been dancing with someone, up at Huber School?"

"No."

"Nate Isaac! Are you blushing?"

He laughed softly, his eyes darting.

She took him by the hand and led him to their secret place in the timber. "All this time, I really thought you had your sights on Vera," she said.

"You must be joking. She was just someone new for us to look at. I told you long ago." Suddenly, he realized she wasn't the same schoolgirl he'd always known. Instead of punching him in the arm, she leaned in close and touched her nose to his. They sat together in the timber until nightfall. Two owls called out to each other mournfully.

"Do you remember all the poetry you used to read me?"

"Yes, I do. I keep it here," he said, pointing to his heart. "Sometimes when I'm out behind the plow, and can't keep going, I remember one. Helps me make it through the day."

"Really," she said, leaning back.

"Maybe it's weird, but sometimes when I can't sleep, I see you. I imagine you're looking down at me from the ceiling."

"That's strange," she said, trying to stifle a laugh.

"You think so?" He sounded a bit wounded.

"That you seeing me hanging up there like a ghost, or something."

"I don't actually see you; I just imagine you there. So you never think of me while you're away?"

"Of course I do. I send you letters, remember?"

He leaned over and kissed her. It was only the second time their lips had met. "Come back tomorrow evening," he said. "I have something to give you."

Nate reached in his pocket the next night and pulled out a small, pearl-handled pistol.

"Why are you giving this to me?" she asked.

"For protection. I worry about you being out there by yourself. Stick it in your purse. It belonged to my grandma."

"I really shouldn't."

"You've already had a few close calls," he said. "The fellas in Kansas City might be harder to push away. This'll slow them down, so you can get away." Nate drew the hammer back, aimed at a tree twenty or so yards away, and dry-fired. Then he dropped six bullets in her hand and gently folded it closed. His big, calloused hand was wrapped around her small, soft one. "Only use it when you need to."

She sat silent, not knowing what to say.

"Look, I won't be there to take care of you, and I need to know you'll be okay."

"All right," she said, finally grateful. "I appreciate your concern."

"You've probably got your sights on someone with more ambition, but I do care for you, Jennie."

"Do you think you're not good enough for me?" She paused to hear his answer, but none came. "You do, don't you?"

"I know you want to be somewhere far from here. I'll probably live and die right here, working the land the rest of my life." He picked up a handful of dirt and let it sift through his fingers.

"I feel bad because I don't have anything to give you."

"It's okay."

"No, it's not," she said, pressing her cheek against his. The summer night was warm and humid, but her throat was cool to the touch. She leaned back into the dogtooth violets, now gleaming like diamonds in the moonlight, pulling him close to her. And they began to kiss.

CHAPTER 18

The Big Town

When her family made their tearful farewell at the one-room depot, Jennie's hair was perfectly pinned up beneath the big, round hat Maggie had given her as a going-away present. The trip from Perry to Kansas City in an open railway car nearly spoiled it.

Thomas let it be known that he did not approve of his unmarried daughter going off to live alone in the city. Mary, on the other hand, struggled somewhere between exuberance and mild embarrassment. When her friends asked questions, Mary told them that her daughter was doing something groundbreaking, and they all should be proud. Jennie was showing the same kind of courage it took for her family to pick up and move from Ohio to Kansas.

Her mother had known for some time that Jennie was different, not the typical young woman who followed tradition. Clearly, she became infatuated with young men she thought could possibly take her someplace in society. Mary seldom heard the girl express any maternal desire. Whatever was there seemed erased by watching Luie painfully bury her firstborn.

Jennie sat on a wooden seat in the third car back from the coal tender, facing the engine. She took great care not to let her eyes meet any strangers'. The railcar was only half full. Tense excitement rose from her toes. Was it because she wasn't accustomed to the speed, or because she realized she was truly on her own?

When the great Union Pacific steam engine whistle blew right through her, she felt her insides might drop. A lanky conductor walked past. He shifted his weight back and forth with the swaying of the train, asked for her ticket and punched it. As he stood there waiting, he brushed against her slightly. Then she saw the ring on his finger.

"Going to K.C. Been there before?" he asked politely. She shook her head. "Well, it's rather lively. Just visiting?" Again, she shook her head. "Then you'll be needing a place to stay." He turned her ticket over, pulled a pen out of his dark blue jacket and wrote down an address. "Ask for Ida. She's my sister. Owns a boarding house for railroaders, but occasionally takes in young ladies. You'd be on a separate floor, of course."

She smiled as he handed back her ticket. "Thank you," she said, barely above a whisper.

Everything looked different from the train. The names of the towns the conductor called along the way seemed familiar, but she recognized nothing. All she could see were the backs of buildings, except when they crossed a main street. The heat was unbearable. She savored the pockets of cool air as they went across creek bridges and rode through canopies of trees. After dozing a bit, she leaned out the window. All she could see was still, algae-covered water. *Clickety-clack, clickety-clack,* the steel wheels and silvery rails sang in a lighthearted song together. Then a long tree branch reached out and slapped her face through the open window. She jumped back into her seat, her heart leaping from her chest.

"Next stop, Kan-sas Ci-ty!" the conductor bellowed. Jennie took off her hat and patted her hair in place. The train's gentle rocking was beginning to make her nauseous. She'd be grateful to step out on solid ground.

The train slowed before it pulled into a dark tunnel underneath the station. It was cooler, here. She stuck her satchel under one arm and lined up behind the other passengers waiting to get off.

Everywhere, men were walking fast, like ants. Plenty came to offer help. One took her hand as she climbed off the train. Another took her bags to the waiting room. More people than she'd ever seen at one time were going in all directions, pulled by invisible schedules, jobs and destinations waiting elsewhere, either in the downtown area or miles down the line. Crying children and strangers unfamiliar with the process of boarding and deboarding the train stood awkwardly in the flow of traffic. She sighed heavily.

"Amazing, isn't it?" a voice said, nearby.

She looked up and saw a huge clock on the wall. She was having a hard time, trying to think, think, think in all this chaos.

Genevieve "Jennie" Hurley as a young woman.
Hurley Family photo

What had the conductor said? Walk to the front of the train, up the stairs, to the right, and into the waiting room. Beyond that was the ticket counter, the lunchroom. No, she wasn't planning to eat, but it was a good place to find a driver to take her to the boarding house the conductor had offered. Impossible to find a carriage right after a train pulled into the station.

Who was this voice of distraction, the one she wanted to reach out and push away? Once again, it asked the same question: "I said, it's amazing, isn't it?" She felt her shoulder being touched, and instinctively turned. It was a wide, strong hand, much like her younger brother's. Only this one was well-manicured and soft. Her eyes turned up, barely visible beneath her hat.

"I'm sorry. Did I startle you?" The man was dressed in white.

Was she obligated to respond? She wondered. What was proper, here in the city? She hated feeling so ill-prepared, so vulnerable. All right, she decided: mutter something quickly, then on with it. However, she dared not take her eyes off her destination, for then she would truly be lost. She looked up at the stranger abruptly and smiled. "Did you say something?" she asked. There was no mistaking the rush in her voice.

"I'm sorry. I don't mean to delay you," he started. His shoulders were broad and his jaw mirrored the same strength. "It looked as though you might need some help."

"And being the hero that you are, you had to stop and ask," she said with a bite at the end.

He opened his mouth, not knowing what to say. Then he put his hands down to his side and smiled. "There's… much more to you than what appears," he guessed precisely.

"I'm sorry, Mr….." Her eyelids fluttered.

"Gilluly. First name William, but folks call me Hunt."

"Well, Mister Gadooley, or whatever, if you're set on accomplishing a good deed today, then I would tell you to just pass me by. I'm sure that plenty of other ladies are looking to be rescued. Now, if you'll excuse me." She really thought that was enough to get rid of him, but she was capable of being cooler.

He touched her arm, and she looked down at his hand this time as if it were leprous. "Pardon me, but it seems like this is new territory for you." He looked around the platform. The crowd was thinning. No one was headed her way.

"That's no concern of yours."

"Can I just say that you have the most incredible brown eyes I've ever seen?"

She sighed in exasperation. So much, that the baggageman could read her body language. "Ma'am? May I help you? Is this man bothering you?"

"I simply want to be on my way."

"Sorry, sir; the lady doesn't need your help." And with that formal invite to leave, the stranger tipped his hat and walked away.

"Anyone you know?" the baggageman asked, picking up the handle of her trunk.

She shook her head.

"Plenty of menfolk keep a watch out for new ladies, here at the station," he explained. "Looks like he barely gave you time to step off the train!"

She was not amused.

"Next time, pretend he doesn't exist. Run right over him, if you must."

"Thank you for your help." She'd lost sight of where she was supposed to go. Instead, her eyes followed the flash of white walking away from her, weaving in and out of the crowd. She noted how his legs tapered off as slender and shapely as a woman's. And immediately she liked this about him.

Smoky darkness billowed out of the first door she opened. Clearly this wasn't the luncheonette, but she was tired of fighting the crowd in the great waiting room. A sign over the door read "Gents Only." Jennie stood at the double-wide threshold, satchel in hand, trunk standing behind her. She might find a driver here, the baggageman told her, but don't expect much.

After she handed him a tip, she could feel the eyes inside fall on her. The jumbled conversations and clack of billiard balls quieted. Surely, she wasn't planning to enter the deep abyss. They waited and watched. "Someone in here want to give me a ride?" The request came forcefully, strong, determined.

Chair legs scraped the sticky wooden floor as a handful of men backed away from tables. The only bright light came from the bar, illuminating a bartender's bald head, making him look rather heavenly.

A boy no older than 14 leapt from his place before the older men could even stand up. They remembered what it was like to be young, and sighed.

"Got a real nice buggy outside for ya!" Throwing his shoulders back and standing with his feet farther apart than necessary, he barely stood as tall as Jennie. "This all you got?" he asked, motioning to the trunk.

"Yes," she said, wanting to explain how the baggageman twice his size had moaned when he lifted it. Still, she knew he was performing for the big audience behind him. "I'm sorry it's so heavy."

"Ah, it's nothing. I can carry it." As he juggled to put the trunk on his back, she tried to help steady it, coaxing without touching. He was creating a scene now, and she was a part of it.

"Name's Mac," he said, trying to thrust out his hand at the same time. "Jimmy Mac." Of the four carriages lined up at the stone hitching posts just outside the depot's castle-sized front doors, Jennie easily guessed which belonged to Mr. Mac: the one that was well worn, dismal, and not the least bit sturdy. With a well-placed hurl, he landed the trunk onto the back of his rickety rig.

She could see horsehair and a rusty spring jutting up through the upholstered seat. There was no top to keep out the rain. To think she'd have to pay for this transport.

"Something wrong, ma'am?" What Jimmy lacked in accommodations, he made up for in charm and honest intent. With his help she climbed up into the carriage, positioning herself awkwardly so as not to tear her new dress. Then she noticed a hole in the floorboard. Water bugs scattered across a puddle underneath.

"Where we headed this afternoon?" he called back without looking. Once he climbed aboard, he tightly grasped the reins.

She opened her satchel and pulled out the ticket the trainman had written on. "Twelfth and Lorraine," she said. She carefully checked to see where her revolver was. It gave her an extra dose of courage, just knowing it was there. If someone caught her off guard, she supposed the weight of it in her bag could bring them down with one good swing.

"Don't worry; I won't talk the whole way," the boy said. "Most people don't care much for me or my whistling."

"Not at all," she encouraged. "In fact, you can tell me all about the city, along the way."

"The city, it is!" He smiled. It was just the request he was waiting for. Jimmy filled the next ten minutes with as much life as the fairytale she'd dreamed of.

CHAPTER 19

A Change of Scenery

Freshly laundered clothing fluttered on a line between two buildings. Jennie stood on the sidewalk in front of them. Both were made of brick. They seemed to be the same two- or three-storied buildings she'd passed on her ride to get here.

She cursed herself. Why hadn't she arranged to stay with someone she knew? Because that was her mother's idea, and she was no child. She could find her own way. However it turned out, she would make the most of it. She left her trunk on the curb and climbed the stairs. A door was open, and the hallway wasn't empty.

"Good day to you," someone said. She recognized the man from the train station with slender legs, dressed in white. "That yours?" he asked, looking down at her trunk.

"Yes," she barely breathed out, realizing it would go nowhere unless she let someone help her.

"Didn't we meet—"

"Do you—"

"Live here? Yes. Should I apologize for our first meeting? Or maybe you prefer I just get out of the way."

Since Jimmy and his wagon were gone, she had no choice. "Of course not. The conductor said I might find a room here."

"At this boarding house?" He smiled. "Did he tell you it was for trainmen?"

"Yes, but he said his sister runs it."

"That she does, but I'm afraid the conductor was leading you astray. This isn't someplace for a lady like you."

She sighed, looking back at the trunk. Tears stung her eyes.

"Look, I'm sorry if I startled you, back at the station. I've got a room here. Now, before you get the wrong idea, I'm not suggesting we stay there at the same time. A friend of mine has a room down the street. I'm sure he'll let me stay a day or two, until you can find something more decent."

All of a sudden, she wanted to trust him. She clutched her satchel tightly, feeling the pistol inside.

He put out his hand to calm her. "I can understand if you don't want to take me up on the offer, but to be fair, you're kind of in a fix. And I'm in a position to help. Let me do this one favor, to make up for the misunderstanding."

"Only if your story is true."

"That I live here?"

"Yes, and that other roomers are trainmen."

"Fair enough. Let me introduce you to the woman who owns the place."

A knock on the door, a brief visit and an explanation from the widow who occupied the main floor confirmed both the stranger's and conductor's stories. Yes, this was a place where trainmen rested in between trips. Sometimes the owner did have extra space, but young women with reputations to protect should look elsewhere.

When the stranger, or Hunt as he reintroduced himself, repeated his solution it seemed the only way. Still wearing his white suit, he dragged her trunk upstairs. Inside, she spotted a lumpy bed with the covers neatly pulled up, a desk with a lantern on top, a nondescript dresser and a dark side chair. Nothing revealed much about its usual occupant. He tipped his hat and bade her good evening.

Jennie pulled a piece of bread from her satchel, sat down on the bed and stuck the gun under her pillow. Then she lit the lamp, trying to keep her eyes open long enough to remember the day's events. She focused on the flame and the closed door until her eyes grew heavy. Before she drifted off to sleep, she got up and turned down the wick. And so began her first night in the city.

She awoke the next morning to a gentle tapping on the door. The room was bathed in misty light. She rose, still dressed in the dusty clothes she'd left home in. Her head ached. Holding it, she opened the door.

"Found you a place to stay." Hunt walked in, holding up a newspaper. "Been up long?"

She shook her head.

"It's almost nine! You didn't rest well."

Stumbling around, she slowly gathered her things. At least he wasn't wearing all white today. But his legs were still thin.

The four-block trip required a carriage again, because of that silly trunk. What should pull up in front of the trainmen's boardinghouse but Jimmy's rundown heap! Hunt watched her face fall. "If this is a repeat of yesterday, I may just go back to Meriden," she muttered.

"Hi there, ma'am. See you're moving about the city again," the boy said.

"You know him?" Hunt asked.

She couldn't bear to speak, so she simply smiled.

Hunt made good on his offer to find a respectable place for her. Immediately Jennie sensed it was tidier, friendlier, safer. This time, two men carried her trunk up the stairs. "Hope you'll be staying longer than a night!" Jimmy jested.

She raised her eyebrows. "Thank you, gentlemen. Now, if you'll let me get settled."

"How about both of you being my guests this evening at a club beneath our city streets?" Hunt offered.

"I'm not sure I'm ready for that much excitement." Hunt's invitation seemed harmless, but she was unsure. She patted the satchel. The hard lump was missing.

Hunt swung the pistol upside down with one finger in the trigger guard. "This what you're looking for?"

"Be careful with that; it's loaded!" She reached out to grab it but he pulled it just out of her reach. Then he took a handful of lead from his pocket.

"No, it's not." He looked at Jimmy and winked. "Now we can do whatever we want."

"No one would suspect a thing." The boy flashed an ornery grin.

"Whatever it is, just go ahead and get it over with," she said, defeated.

"All right, then." Hunt loaded each chamber. She held her breath. Jimmy looked a little nervous. "Here." He closed the revolver and handed it to him.

"Me? I won't do it."

Hunt laughed. "All I'm asking is for you to be our driver and protection tonight."

"When can I get my gun back?" Jennie asked.

"After supper."

Few places in Kansas City would serve liquor to a woman; Hunt knew every one of them. He appeared to be a regular at the saloon located at 931 Broadway, for when he entered the glass doors of Fitzpatricks, the maitre d' silently escorted the unlikely trio past an innocent crowd of diners, down the stairs to a long, narrow room.

They descended into a white fog of cigar smoke that clung to the ceiling. Tonight's patrons were mostly well-dressed businessmen trying to unwind at the end of the workday. They threw back short, heavy glasses of liquor with one hand and jabbed at their steaks with the other. On their laps sat women who laughed a little too loudly and were dressed too brightly to be their wives. Jennie could guess what kind of place this was. No one looked at her or the teenage boy questioningly. They were simply another tableful of patrons.

On a raised platform, a piano player pounded out a rollicking ragtime. Hunt pulled out a chair for Jennie to sit in. Jimmy sat next to her, wide eyed and taking in the scene. He'd heard of such places but never got past the front doors.

Hunt yelled into the waiter's ear. After a few minutes, he reappeared with a bottle of whiskey and three glasses. Jennie covered hers and shook her head.

"Just a little," Hunt coaxed. She took a sip, and the straight shot burned her throat. Jimmy downed his and pointed at his glass to have another.

There was little said between them, for one could hardly hear above the music. Occasionally the piano player slowed things down with an Irish immigrant's ballad, something mournful about missing his homeland. They were served a full-course meal on fine dishes and table linens.

After a few bites, the music stopped and the piano player took a break. Jennie dabbed the corners of her mouth with a cloth napkin. "How can a railroader like yourself afford such a fine meal?"

Jimmy watched her place the napkin back on her lap, then pulled his out of the top of his shirt.

"Did I say I worked for the railroad?" Hunt asked.

"No."

"You thought that because I stayed at the boardinghouse."

"So, what do you do for a living?" she pressed.

"A little of this, a little of that." He winked at Jimmy.

"I don't care, as long as he buys our steaks!" the boy exclaimed.

The liquor and food went on a tab covered by Hunt's brother, Ross. He occupied an office high above the streetcar line in the Met Life Building. An attorney, Ross mingled with some of the most powerful men in town. After a conversation with Hunt, he agreed to send a letter of recommendation on Jennie's behalf to the school superintendent. As it turns out, the family had spent some time in Jefferson County. Ross knew people that Jennie knew.

The infamous trunk moved again, this time to a townhouse apartment across from Ross and his wife's home. Hunt wore down the carpet, walking back and forth between the two living spaces.

CHAPTER 20

Autumn Love

"What are you reading, Mother?" Ernest was leaning on the back of Mary's chair, which was about to tumble backwards.

"Stop it! You're going to land me on the floor." She clutched the chair's arm with her one good hand and planted a foot solidly on the floor. "I'm reading a letter from Jennie."

Mary pushed herself too hard, working to prepare a family feast that Christmas. Four days later, she suffered a stroke that affected her left arm.

"What does she say?" Ernest asked.

"Everything sounds fine. She's being paid to sing professionally, in addition to working as a store clerk."

"Where's she singing?"

"Doesn't say, but she sounds happy."

Mary worried about Jennie and wished she were home to help. However, the girl needed to carve out a life of her own. She wasn't like Mary's other daughters who dreamed of getting married and having children. Thomas, on the other hand, wanted to go bring Jennie back home. Mary knew this would only make things worse.

"She's worked so hard to get to Kansas City," Mary pleaded with him. "Surely we can manage without her."

"What do I know about keeping a house, Mary Elizabeth, and what does your son know, either? Besides, the boy wants to go to college, himself."

Ernest leaned on the back of his mother's chair yet again, looking over her shoulder at what she was reading. *If only he knew how much that irritated me,* she thought. Mary turned and looked up at him. He was becoming a man. She'd noticed his forearms becoming quite muscular, lately. She looked out the window. "One day,

Ernest, my body will have enough, and then I'll be gone."

"What makes you say that?"

"I just want to prepare you. We've had the least amount of time together. Soon, you'll be off to college, or you'll settle down and start a family. In either case, you'll need to find someone to take care of your father."

"One of the girls can."

"Where? In their house? You know he'd never leave this place. It's the only home he's known, since leaving Ireland. I imagine he'll keep farming until he drops behind the plow." Mary sighed. "I just thought I'd be here to get him ready for his funeral."

"Why wouldn't you?"

"I don't want to worry you, but I really haven't felt quite right since the stroke. It's all I can do to get around."

"If you don't think I should go to college, Mom, I won't."

"I want you to. I'm just worried about your dad. Is there a way you could take courses and stay on the farm?"

"I don't think so. Maybe I could go later. I'll have the rest of my life to do it."

"This must be your decision, not mine."

"If it eases your mind, then I'll give you my word. I'll stay as long as he needs me."

"You're a good boy." She patted his hand. "You've always been my sweetest. You know what's odd?" she asked. "Jennie never mentions where she's singing. Wouldn't it be nice to ride over and see her?"

"You mean, go surprise her?"

"Why not? If she's doing as well as she says, we ought to." Mary picked up the photograph taken of her and Thomas the year before.

"Has Dad ever talked much about his family back home?"

"Just that he was named for his dad, and his ma was named Nora. And that the people around him thought he should become a priest. There might be some uncles in Australia but everything else seems off limits, even to me."

Ernest placed a small footstool in front of Mary, admiring her delicate needlework on top.

"He was only several years younger than you when he made that trip. Imagine a young boy leaving home alone, sailing across the ocean to a place he'd never been."

"Did he have any family here, when he arrived?"

"There was talk of an aunt but we never hear from her. He's never asked to send a letter or Christmas card."

The back door slammed, breaking the conversation. "The past is the past," Thomas said from behind the kitchen door. "I'll not tell either of you, again."

"How long you been listening, Love?" Mary asked.

"Long enough."

"Dad, wouldn't it be nice to hear from your family?" Ernest asked.

"All of the Metzgers in Jefferson County aren't enough for the lot of you?" Thomas looked sidelong at Mary. He was smiling now, waving a wooden spoon.

"Thomas Hurley, what are you doing in my kitchen?" she chided.

"I'll help," Ernest offered.

She shook her head. "Two men rattling around with the dishes."

"I told you, Mother. I'll take care of things."

As the summer evening gave way to autumn's door, the sun rested just above the top of the hill, spreading orange light across the Delaware River Valley. The boardwalk creaked with each of Thomas' steps. Mary sat on the porch and struggled to pull a shawl up around her shoulders. No matter how hard she tried, her left arm just wouldn't cooperate tonight. She felt someone helping her, and reached up to touch Thomas' hand. He patted her softly and let his hand linger there.

"Are the horses tucked in for the night?" she whispered as he leaned back against the porch post.

"Aye. Molly's ready to foal. Could be any time." He looked up through the branches of the giant maple tree as it gently swayed in the breeze.

"I wish I could help," she said regretfully.

"It's a man's job."

"Remember how we used to sit out in the barn all night and wait for the new ones to arrive?"

"About the only time we got to talk without being interrupted," he noted. "Remember how sore you'd get, after all that tugging?"

"Imagine how the mother felt."

"Aye, guess you'd know."

"I do miss bringing babies into the world, Thomas, and being there for mothers when they deliver. The moment a child's born, it's as if God himself has reached down and touched us with his hand."

"Sure, and it's a blessing."

"Not once have I regretted what I went through, to give our children life."

"Then the real work began."

"Most weren't difficult. Except Maggie and Jennie. It was hard getting them here…."

"And it's still hard." They spoke together at the same time, laughing at their perfect timing.

"I wish things had been better between us, before she left." Mary remembered how determined Jennie was to go by herself, and the argument she had with her father, insisting she didn't need his help.

"She'll live higher and farther than we ever dreamed," he said.

"I think she'll do fine."

"Just wish she'd settle down."

"If she got married, do you think she'd really be happy? She doesn't like anyone telling her what to do. What did we do to make her so stubborn?"

"Maybe it's the way God made her," he supposed. "She couldn't wait to leave home."

"You know, I just don't understand that," Mary said. "To me, this farm is the closest thing to heaven."

"I've tried to make it nice for you and the children."

"It's lovely, Thomas. I've loved our life." She looked up at him and watched a tiny drop of water roll down his cheek. In all their years together, she'd only seen him cry once or twice before. She pretended not to notice, because she knew he'd be embarrassed. "I'd say that we've weathered it pretty well."

"We have, at that," he agreed, then turned to silently wipe away the tear. He was growing more tenderhearted with each passing year.

CHAPTER 21

The Homecoming

Mary suffered a second stroke several months after her first one. Her entire left side was paralyzed. She spent the next four years courageously living with the constant help of Thomas, while Ernest took up most of the farm duties. Seldom did she complain. It was said that she still "ruled the roost," even from her wheelchair. Finally she weakened, and ten days later Mary Elizabeth Metzger Hurley, mother of sixteen children, died at 3 a.m. on August 24, 1914. She was 65.

Her funeral services were held outside the farmhouse. Black crepe paper covered the front door. Mirrors were covered as well, a typical mourning custom. Neighbors, friends and relatives came to pay their respects. Each man received a black armband to wear.

The Rev. Janssen of the Meriden Methodist Episcopal Church conducted the service. "We owe our debt to our mothers," he began, "and the best way to pay that debt would be to live such lives as our mothers would have us live, and to promise to meet them in heaven. In the words of the poet, 'Tell Mother I'll be there.'"

Hunt followed Jennie from the car as she slipped into a chair beside Ernest. Four young people stood and sang "Abide with Me." Jennie gazed at the spray of flowers on Mary's coffin. Ernest tried to catch his sister's eye. They were both thinking the same thing: it should've been their voices singing, rising over the meadow, sending their mother off to her new home. How many funerals had they sung together, for other families?

"(These flowers) will soon fade away like all of earthly things, but the flowers of the grave which bloomed in the soul of this departed mother will never fade," *The Meriden Ledger* later reported the Rev. Janssen saying. "The influence of true mothers lingers with us not only to bless and brighten our pathway, but to guide us, like a star of hope, through the battles of life into the eternal haven of peace.

"Thank God for Christian mothers. They are the best friends we have. They are the bulwark of a nation's strength. We voice the sentiment of the poet who wrote this verse titled 'Only One Mother':

Hundreds of stars in the pretty sky,
Hundreds of shells on the shores together;
Hundreds of birds that go singing by,
Hundreds of bees in the sunny weather.
Hundreds of dewdrops to greet the dawn,
Hundreds of lambs in the wild clover;
Hundreds of butterflies out on the lawn,
But only one mother the wide world over.

"To the comfort of children and grandchildren may it be said, 'Mother is not dead; mother has gone to her eternal home to live forever and ever.'"

The funeral processed up out of the valley, north to a hilltop in Meriden. Each of the children and grandchildren took a flower from Mary's casket, whispering their goodbyes.

As Hunt led Jennie away from the graveside, holding her shoulders to steady her, something caught her eye. Jennie's old friend Nate was leaning up against a Douglas fir, hands in his pockets. He must have borrowed a suit for the occasion. He nodded at her, then caught Hunt's eye. Hunt glared back coldly as they passed and made their way back to the automobile.

Nate looked down at his grubby fingernails. He knew he was not of their caliber. Ernest had told him that Jennie's boyfriend sold new Ford motorcars, and she had become the music director for the Kansas City, Kansas, school district. Jennie had learned it paid, quite literally, to know the right people.

They stood next to a shiny black car. Nate wished he were standing in Hunt's place, comforting the only girl he ever loved. Neither of them were kids anymore, now in their mid-30s. As Jennie looked up to kiss Hunt, Nate could see the crinkles at the corner of her eyes, the lightening of her hair where it met her face.

She was starting to age. Her fresh grief only accented these visible signs.

And then what amazed Nate most happened that day as he stood unaware. Hunt walked Jennie to the car her father was riding in, shook Mr. Hurley's hand and walked away. Jennie did not look Hunt's way as he drove off. She simply got in next to her father. Someone shut the door behind her, and the long line of cars and carriages slowly pulled away from the spot where Mary's casket lay.

Mary and T.A. Hurley, later in life. Hurley Family photo

CHAPTER 22

A Carload of Trouble

1920

Why Jennie came home was a question everyone longed to know the answer to. They knew she had a quick temper. Certainly she wouldn't be able to keep up the same standard of living. Her income in the city was greater than most men living in the country. Now, she was back to being a farmer's daughter. Now, her challenges were the mundane chores of cooking and keeping house. Ernest would stay on, as he promised Mary.

The house filled with a flurry of activity. Jennie dusted, laundered and aired out everything until her shoulders and back ached. Two of her favorite men were arriving. They weren't the regular courters from Kansas City, who appeared regularly on the front porch and sent her lengthy letters, but her brothers Eli and Tom, and their families.

An open car bounced down the road and around the corner to the homeplace. It was loaded with Eli and the kids. One of them excitedly announced their arrival by continually squeezing a large, bell-shaped horn.

"Dad, they're here!" Jennie leaned against the back bedroom door. The old man opened his eyes and groaned a little as he rose from his cot. Jennie took off her apron and hung it on a hook in the kitchen. She pushed up her hair, regathering the loose strands with a tortoise shell comb.

"You look fine," Thomas commented as he watched her smooth the wrinkles in a white pinafore. "You're still the best-looking woman in the county." He smiled at her in encouragement.

"Oh, go on now," she blushed.

"Shall I say more nice things?"

"You make me feel silly."

"Like the schoolgirl of yesteryear."

The front door flew open and banged against the wall, causing the glass to rattle. "Ernest, how many times have I told you?" the old man startled.

"Sometimes he's such an ox," Jennie whispered under her breath.

Ernest paid no attention, for he was overcome with excitement. "We've got company!"

Third son Eli entered the house with three of his children behind.

"And who would you be bringing with you?" Thomas asked, greeting the little ones.

"Oh, Grandpa," Maude said. "You know who we are!"

"Little lost urchins, making your way across Kansas? Looking for biscuits, I suppose."

"They're as red as the dickens!" Jennie exclaimed as she saw little Harold's sunburnt ears and cheeks. She shot a scolding glance at Eli.

"Daddy let us drive with the top down!" Claude said proudly.

"Did Daddy's brains bake in the sun, on the way?" Jennie asked with a half-smile.

"Hi, Sis." Eli said, reaching out to embrace her.

"Hello, you," she answered, giving in to his brotherly affection. "Where's the rest?"

"You mean Luie and the little ones? It's a tight squeeze in that car, especially on a warm day."

"What about Beulah?"

"She's at home, helping Luie with Phyllis."

"Hello, Dad." Eli greeted his father with a handshake and gentle clasp on the arm. "Are they here, yet?"

"Tom and his new bride?" the old man asked. "They'll be along tomorrow. Driving in from Dodge."

"I thought they were in Colorado."

"Tom was," Ernest explained. "Been working at a sawmill in Yampa, but drove down to Dodge to get married. That's where his wife lived."

"Hey, we've got a boarder," Ernest interrupted.

"Who?" Eli inquired.

"Calvin Barry."

"No kidding."

"You kids go out and play, so we can visit," Eli directed. "Where's Andy and George?"

"Don't you ever write to anyone?" Ernest joked.

"No. Luie doesn't have time to keep up. Too busy with the kids."

"Well, Andy's over in Kaw Township, working for Mr. Ingle," Thomas offered. "George is farming out in Colorado. He does that during the summer."

"You really believe all those stories that he and Tom tell about living up in the mountains?" Eli asked.

Ernest laughed. "You can never be sure."

"Oh, I believe it, all right," the old man said softly, his voice weakening with age.

"That's right, Dad's been up there. Knows all about mining and hunting," Ernest pointed out.

"But I also know your brothers, too." He smiled broadly.

From the parlor came the innocent plinking from a piano that revealed an unaccomplished player.

"That'd be Maude," Eli said. "She's dying to learn how to play."

"I could give her a few pointers," Jennie offered.

"Would you? If it's no bother."

"Heavens no. I've taught most of the children in this county." Jennie excused herself from the room while the men sat around the table, catching up. In the background Maude's slow-paced, unsure notes filled the air, repeating over and over.

"Reckon Tom will take his bride back to Steamboat?" Eli asked.

"He's been working on a cabin close to town," Ernest answered. "I know his heart's not been into railroading, lately."

"That's for sure. The boy's got the mountains in his blood. Just like George," Thomas observed.

"It's quite a-ways up there, isn't it?" Eli said.

"Yes, but now a man can get to Steamboat Springs by train, through Denver. Getting across the pass was pretty tough until recently. Suppose that's why your brothers became such good skiers and snowshoers."

George and Tom, aka "Ted" or "T.J.," carved a life high up in the mountains northwest of the town that later became known as a skiing mecca. Before they were establishing skiing as a sport down in the valley, the Hurley brothers were doing it out of necessity. They spent winters holed up in a tiny cabin, venturing out into Routt County when the snow let up enough so they could track deer, elk, and other wild game.

When tracking became monotonous, they'd load up their gear and scour the hills for caves. If they were lucky, they could find a hibernating cinnamon bear; their adrenaline surged in anticipation. It was not a sport for the weak-hearted. One of them would grab a hunting knife and crawl into a cave quietly while the other stood at the opening. Rifle in hand, he would be poised to fire once the bear had been rudely awakened. Of course, the first man in had to back out quickly so the second could finish the job.

This scheme worked well except for once, when Tom crawled in and George misfired. Tom ended up with a bullet slug near his collar bone. It stayed there the rest of his life. Years later his little boy Lucius would play with it, feeling it underneath the skin with his fingers as he sat on his lap. When his dad would tell him to stop it, he would ask, "What is it?" Tom would answer, "Ah, that's where George shot me." At least both the brothers had made it out alive. The same couldn't be said for the bear. When they propped it up for a photo, it stood as tall as the men.

According to a newspaper account, they got one of these bears up at Crystal Peak. They tied the big, hairy creature onto a sled and skied down with it, to Steamboat. There, they traded it for supplies at the trading post and at F.M. Light & Sons, a store handed down through the generations. It is still located on Lincoln Avenue.

In those parts of Colorado near the Great Divide, George and Tom were known as drinkers and brawlers. However, they probably weren't much tougher than other miners and hunters of the day. Just like their kinfolk back in Kansas, they quarreled a lot. One winter, they had a good fight and refused to speak or apologize to each other. They communicated by writing notes on the back of canned good labels. When spring arrived, every meal was a surprise; they could only guess what was inside each can.

Their stubbornness likely kept them alive. On his way to Steamboat to trade pelts one spring, Tom was caught in an avalanche and had to rely on his senses to save him. He was trapped beneath several feet of snow. After a while, he heard water running under him; as luck or the Lord would have it, he was lying above a frozen stream. Somehow, he found one of his ski poles. With the end of it, he pushed down and poked through a layer of ice. Eventually he could lower his body into the water. This gave him enough room to work above and dig himself out. When he finally reached Steamboat, observers said he was frozen from head to toe, looking like an abominable snowman.

Summers gave the men a chance to get back to their skills honed in Jefferson County. They closed the cabin for the season and hired on with ranchers down in Yampa Valley. They also worked on farms and with threshing crews. Tom earned a reputation for breaking the most stubborn horses, forming them into dependable workers. If he couldn't train a horse by the time it was a year old, there was little chance of curing its habits. He would flatly tell people they shouldn't expect too much. Nevertheless, his price was the same.

Thomas and Eli's conversation was cut by a scream from the parlor. Eli leapt across the room to find his daughter sitting in tears at the piano. Jennie stood over her, holding a ruler.

"What happened?" he asked. Maude sobbed, holding her hand. "Let me see." He gently cradled the young girl's wrist and eyed a welt rising just above her knuckles. "Jennie, what's going on here?"

"She wasn't holding her hands correctly. I must have told her ten times, but she just wouldn't listen."

"I think Maude is through with this lesson. Let's go into the kitchen and get some ice for that." He glared at Jennie. "Why do you do things like this? I know you don't have any kids of your own, but you could show a little more patience."

"I thought she wanted my help."

"Yes, but not punishment. I'll discipline my own children, thank you very much!"

"All right, then. I'm sorry."

"Now I don't know if I can trust you with her tonight."

"Whatever do you mean?"

"I thought you two would share a bed, but now I'm not so sure."

"Really, Eli. She was making more of it than it was. Just one tap on the hand was all. Look, I'll apologize to her and everything will be fine."

"I was hoping the two of you could get along."

Jennie put up both hands. "Eli, I promise. I'll behave from now on."

CHAPTER 23

In the Midnight Hour

"Maude, you'll sleep with me tonight." Jennie pulled the curtains closed as the sun disappeared over the hill west of the farm, fading the bright colors of the day. An hour after supper, Jennie took Maude aside and gently apologized to her. They spent the rest of the evening playing ragtime music on the Victrola. "Eli, you can sleep with Claude and Harold in the guest room across the hall," Jennie said.

He looked at Maude for her reaction. "You okay with that?" he asked. She nodded. "Who sleeps in Momma's old room?"

"I do," Jennie responded. "Dad sleeps downstairs, next to the kitchen."

"Don't you feel a bit strange, sleeping in her bed?"

"Because she died there? No. She could've been downstairs or sitting at the kitchen table. Should we never eat again, if that were the case, or walk around the house, just to keep from going through the dining room?"

He didn't answer, irritated that her tone was already sharp again. Where was the playful Jennie he once knew?

Maude crawled into the feather bed, surrounded by thick blankets so that only her face showed. She was still a bit scared of Jennie, although her father assured her everything was okay.

"You cold?" Jennie asked with a tinge of concern.

"I shouldn't be, because it's May."

"You must be chilling from your sunburn," Jennie concluded. "Just wrap up all warm and tight." She tucked the blankets around her.

"But they're scratchy," Maude complained.

"Would you rather be cold, and get sick from shivering?" Jennie moved to a chair in front of the mirror, pulling pins from her hair and letting it dangle loosely, just below her waistline.

"You have pretty hair," Maude remarked, somewhat in awe.

"I suppose your Momma cuts hers short."

"Yes. Did it used to be long, like yours?"

"Before all her babies came. Before little Theodore died. Poor child. Guess you've heard that story."

"Daddy says we shouldn't talk about it, since it upsets Momma."

"How old are you?"

"Fourteen."

"Ever kissed a boy?" she asked, turning the lamp down as she started to get into her bedclothes.

"Once, but he was a cousin."

"Doesn't count then. You will, someday. Probably a schoolboy. I used to teach school, you know."

Maude nodded.

"Taught all around here, then in Kansas City. Even up in Des Moines. You know where that's at?"

"Iowa?"

"Yes." She climbed in next to Maude and turned the wick down on the lamp. There were surrounded by darkness.

"Aunt Jennie?"

"Yes, dear."

"I can't see you."

"Put up your hand." She did so, timidly. Jennie grabbed ahold of it. "Here I am! You're not scared, are you?"

"No. Just not used to this big, old house."

"You know, your Dad and Momma used to live here when it was just a few rooms. If I remember right, you were born in this house!"

"I don't remember."

"I wouldn't expect you to. Would you like to go to church in the morning? Maybe your Dad would drive us over to Thompsonville. I teach Sunday school."

"For children?"

"For young ladies your age."

"But I don't know anyone."

"You'll make new friends. It's always good to stretch yourself."

The starched pillowcase and woolen blanket kept scratching Maude's cheeks but eventually she fell sleep. In the middle of the night she woke with a chill. When she reached over to find Jennie, the bed was empty beside her.

Maude rose and went to the window, her nose pressed against the pane. She could see the headlights of a car and somebody dash out from the house. A car door opened, then closed. Then the vehicle sped away.

"They're here!" Jennie called from the kitchen. She was standing at the sink, washing breakfast dishes. Maude was sitting at the table, polishing silver. She hadn't heard Jennie come back upstairs, but in the morning she acted as though nothing had happened.

"Aunt Jennie, did you know you have a hole in your dress?"

"Oh no! Where?" She whirled around, soap bubbles flying everywhere. "Is it bad? Does it show much?"

"Only when you lean over the sink."

"It'll have to do. This is my best dress. Anyhow, it's too late to change. Tom and his new wife are here. Do me a favor and help me make sure Grandpa is ready."

Maude followed her to the parlor.

"Let's tie that," Jennie said, tending to Thomas' bowtie. Then she squared the shoulders of his freshly pressed shirt. "You look fine. Oh, where's Ernest? Ernest!" she yelled, running to the back door.

"I'm coming," he answered, trotting in from the barn.

"Still in your overalls, I see." She looked down at his dirty knees.

"You didn't expect me to wear my Sunday best to do chores, did you?"

"No, just hurry up. They're here already. You do want to look presentable, right?"

"Yes."

"Then run upstairs, lickety-split." He took the steps two at a time.

"Jennie, you've got to stop treating your brother like a boy. He's a man, now."

"Daddy, we don't even have time to get into that. Besides, if he's a man, why doesn't he start acting like one?"

"Hullo there!" a strong voice called from outside. "Anybody home?"

Jennie opened the door and greeted her brother Tom with a warm embrace. "Hi, Love," she said loud enough so his new wife could hear. Jennie kissed his cheek and accidentally knocked off his derby. "Oh, sorry!"

He smiled at the two women nervously. "Dance with me, Jen." He took her hands, swaying back and forth with her in his arms.

"Tom!" she exclaimed in surprise. "Why, there's not even any music!"

Maude watched and giggled.

"Sweet Genevieve, my Genevieve..." Tom began to sing.

"Please stop. This is not the place or the time!"

He stopped suddenly and stepped back, pretending to be mad. "Jennie Hurley, are you saying I'm a poor dancer?"

She had to look at him hard to see if he was serious, then decided he wasn't. "Stop acting so foolish, and introduce me." She gently slapped his lapel.

"This lovely dark-haired woman who's been standing by patiently since we came in the door? Genevieve Hurley, may I present Miss Helen Balch. Mrs. Tom Hurley, I mean!"

"Pleased to meet you," Jennie offered.

"Likewise."

Immediately Jennie noticed how tall the young woman was—almost a head taller than Tom. And so young! She bit her tongue.

"Brought your piano back with you, I see," Tom noticed the dark walnut upright standing beneath the stairway, the cover lifted and ready to play. Two or three music books were open, just as Jennie had left them yesterday evening. Tom led Helen over and pointed to the photos neatly arranged on top. Underneath was a pretty white runner, edged in yellow tatting.

"That's Dad and Mother. When was this picture taken, Jen?"

"I think their fortieth anniversary." Helen looked at the couple in the photo, curious to know what Tom's mother looked like. Mary looked tired from all the children she'd raised. She was glad Tom didn't expect her to have a houseful of babies.

"Where's Dad?" he asked.

"Maybe upstairs to tell the rest that you arrived."

"Who's this pretty young woman?" Tom reached over and touched Maude's cheek.

"Your niece," Jennie explained.

"Lucile?"

"No, Maude."

"You were only as high as my knee, the last time I saw you."

Eli poked his head around the banister at the top of the stairs.

"Come down here, old man!" Tom shouted.

"Somebody call me?" Thomas answered, befuddled.

"You coming down, or you going to make me climb the stairs to see you?"

"Jennie, how long you been home?" Tom had found a place to sit next to his new wife on the sofa. Thomas and Eli sat opposite. Jennie sat back in her mother's rocking chair.

"Since Momma passed away. Came home to help Dad and Ernest with the house and make sure they don't kill each other." Jennie got up and poured some iced tea, then garnished it with a sprig of mint from the garden.

"What do you do for fun these days?" Tom asked.

"I'm studying piano with Miss Whittlesley and voice with Paul Lawless over in Topeka."

"Not a soul around here properly buried unless Jennie and Ernest sing at their funeral," Thomas announced. Helen nodded respectfully.

Tom bragged on his new bride. "Helen plays piano, too," he

said. She lowered her eyes, not used to being in the limelight.

Jennie kept the conversation going. "What do you like to play? Classical?"

"A little of everything. I play for the nickelodeon in Dodge City."

"Oh, can't that run the gamut!" she said, referring to how the music had to match the mood of what was going on in the silent movies. "Must be challenging. I admit, I've only glanced at the music."

"Yes," Helen barely got out.

"And there's so many different pieces to learn. A friend had a book of sheet music that must've been an inch thick! How do you know what to play, and when to play it?"

"I watch the screen while I'm playing. Some players develop a repertoire for each mood."

"Do you have to memorize any of it?"

"Oh yes, but it's fun. What do you play?"

"Mostly classical. Formal nonsense, really: scales and etudes. However, it's wonderful training. Pieces by Schubert, Chopin, Mozart, Verdi. Right now, I'm working on Rachmaninoff's 'Prelude in C-Sharp Minor.'"

"Sounds like ghost music," Thomas interjected.

"Oh Dad, it's wonderful. A genius piece of music that exudes such drama and passion! I can't help but play it with everything in me," she went on, waving her arms.

Helen was taken aback. She'd never seen anyone so enthusiastic over sheet music.

"Her piano is in Dodge," Tom explained, trying to draw attention away from Jennie. "We'll try to move it when we're settled in."

"Who, Helen? She's no wee lassie, is she?" Thomas leaned over and whispered this last part a little too loudly to Eli, who shot back a scolding look.

"He hasn't changed a bit," Tom remarked.

"A heart of gold," Jennie joked.

"So, Helen it is," Thomas started. "Where did you come from?"

"Dodge City. But my family is from Emporia and Fort Scott."

"Ah, bunch of ruffians down there," Thomas growled as he took a sip of iced tea.

"Dad, please," Tom scolded.

"No, he's right," Helen said, trying to be a pleasant daughter-in-law. "In fact, they say my grandfather was shot by some border ruffians in the Civil War."

"You think that was long ago? I was there. Pushed back Price's boys at Westport."

Tom and Eli exchanged knowing glances. "We all know you did your part in the war, Dad. What's for dinner?" Tom said, rubbing his hands together in anticipation. He didn't want his new wife to drown in boredom.

"Your favorite," Jennie said. "Come to the kitchen with me, Helen. I'll show you what I've made."

"We never lost a man, you know," Thomas added a bit late, for most of his captive audience had already left the room.

"I'll round up the kids outside," Eli said.

"I see you brought your little rascals." Tom took a sip of tea.

"They're not so little anymore. Maude and Claude are 14."

"Can't be!"

"Lucile is already out on her own."

"I must be getting old."

"Not too old to have some of your own, I hope. She quite a bit younger than you?" he asked, pointing at Helen with his eyes.

Ernest finally bounded down the stairs. "Brother Tom!"

"Little brother!" The two shook hands. Tom grabbed Ernest's elbow with his free hand. "Mighty pair of muscles you got there. Must be working hard."

"Aye, for the boy he is," Thomas interjected.

"He's no boy, Dad. He's 25. Isn't that right?"

"Yes," Ernest answered.

"The youngest shall always be a lad, don't you know?" Thomas mused.

"What's this I hear?" Jennie poked her head out the kitchen

door. "We were just talking about that boy this morning."

"Go back to your work, woman," Thomas said, feeling strong from having so many men around him. "What does she know, anyway? She got fired from her job."

"Really?" Eli asked. "What a shame."

"Dad, we're not talking about that today," Ernest scowled.

"Shot off her mouth again, that's what she did," Thomas tried explaining.

"You don't even know," Ernest said. "Could've been something else."

"Why do you defend her? She'd as soon take a stick to your backside."

"All right, now," Tom intervened. "Let's calm down. My new wife doesn't need the five-cent tour, if you know what I mean. Let's show her the nice, happy family that we are."

"Is that what we're supposed to be doing?" Eli asked.

"Well it's about time," Thomas said as the two women walked into the dining room carrying a large plate and bowls filled with fried chicken and vegetables.

"Is this your new bride?" Ernest asked, pointing at Helen.

"Well, she's not your new cook!" Tom joked.

"You'll be needing one, if I hear any more remarks about my food." Jennie raised an eyebrow.

"You know I love your cooking, Sis," Ernest made a point to say.

"Yes, this is my wife, Helen." Tom put his hand lovingly around her waist. Ernest noted how she towered over him by almost a foot.

"Glad to have you in our family." Ernest supposed that he and Helen were about the same age.

"Where are those children of yours, Eli?" Jennie asked. "Better tell them to wash up before they come to the table."

"How'd you get one so young?" Eli whispered to Tom as he passed behind him. Helen eyed them suspiciously.

"He wants to know how we met," Tom explained. "When I worked out in Dodge for Santa Fe, I stayed at a boarding house owned by Mrs. Burgland. She had a young daughter who was kind enough to visit me and write while I was in the hospital."

"Was that when you got scalded on the engine?" Ernest asked.

"Yes. When I heard that Helen was about to marry a doctor in Dodge City who had a new car, I got a new suit and proposed before it was too late."

"These two will be following behind you soon," Thomas said, nodding toward Genevieve and Ernest.

"Really?"

"He'd like to think so," Jennie responded.

"You remember Holly Cook?" Ernest asked. "The family that lived northeast of Meriden about three miles? Her father is Charles Cook. Her mother died during the flu epidemic."

"Where'd you meet?"

"A dance at the schoolhouse. Eugene Cook, from the other Cook family, introduced us," he explained to his new sister-in-law.

"Who's your lucky man, Jen?" Tom teased.

"Lon Myers," Thomas answered.

"The farmer who lost his wife?"

"Yes. He'll be a fine husband."

"He's a friend. We go to church sometimes," Jennie explained.

"It's more than that," Thomas said firmly. "They've set a wedding date. And if I don't do anything else before I die, I'll see you walk down that aisle with him."

"Maybe you will, maybe you won't," Jennie said, bowing her head.

"Whatever do you mean?" he asked.

"I get to have the final say in matters as important as this. Don't get any ideas about you being the one to choose who I'll marry. I'm not some fairytale princess, after all!" Her neck had turned beat red and her chest was heaving.

"Jennie," Eli warned. "Please calm down."

"I will not!" she said, standing at her chair. "Your father still hasn't gotten it into his head that I'm a grown woman. I don't need anyone telling me what to do, and when!"

"But you came back home, didn't you, and expected to be taken care of," Thomas responded. "What's a woman your age suited for, except becoming a wife? You've probably waited too long to become a mother." As soon as he spoke, he knew it was the wrong thing.

Eli's children came in the back door. He quickly scurried them back outside.

Jennie doubled up her fists and held them at her side. Then she began pointing a finger at her father. "Old man, you have no idea what you're talking about. You don't know what I've done with my life, what I'm capable of. I ran an entire school district of music teachers. I beat three men out of that position. And I did a damn fine job!"

"They teach women in Kansas City to swear?" Thomas asked boldly, letting the sparks fly.

"If that's what it takes to get your attention! I'll tell you something: this is a different time than when you were young. Women aren't throwing themselves at the feet of just anyone so they can cook and clean. In case you haven't noticed, we can vote, now. Someone must think we have brains enough to make big decisions."

"Who put all these crazy notions in your head?" Thomas wondered aloud.

"I'm not the little girl who left here twenty years ago. I'm a middle-aged woman, and I say who I'll marry, and who I won't!" Then she stormed out the back door.

Everyone was wide eyed. No one made a move for quite some time. The men slowly began to eat in silence. Helen didn't say a word. She got up and moved around the kitchen, trying to find something to occupy her time. When they were done eating, she cleared the table, barely speaking. Tom grabbed her hand as she passed, trying to apologize. Certainly this wasn't how he'd imagined their first trip home.

"Another fine meal served at the Hurley place," Thomas said cynically, wiping his mouth with a napkin, then adding a few words in Gaelic that no one understood. Finally he rose and went to his bedroom, where his cot awaited.

Tom watched until the door closed, then turned to Ernest. "Has it been like this, for long?"

Ernest sighed. "Afraid so. Sometimes it's so bad I have to sleep out in the barn. Dad can't get out like he used to, so he's stuck here with her."

"He really needs to stop meddling in her life," Eli observed.

"He thinks that's the problem. That Mother didn't put her foot down hard enough when she needed to."

"Maybe she's going through the change of life," Helen offered. The men looked at her. "It can change a woman's behavior."

"Is it permanent?" Eli asked.

"No, but sometimes it takes years to pass."

"Wonderful," Ernest said, discouraged.

"Never could handle her temper," Eli recalled.

"She doesn't always make the best of choices," Tom agreed. "Why'd she come back if she had such an important job?"

"Supposedly to take care of Dad and me, and the house. But I don't think that's the whole story. Eva Baker—sister Kate's daughter—was staying here, helping. She was doing a fine job but Jennie insisted she leave. Poor girl. Left suddenly one morning without saying goodbye."

Eva was a slender, pretty girl. Her parents were Kate, the second-eldest Hurley daughter, and George Baker. George lived close to the Hurley farm and worked eighty acres of corn.

"Did Jennie make her leave?" Tom asked. He didn't want to believe his closest sister could be so malicious.

"Wouldn't doubt it," Ernest said. "Kate said Jennie threw Eva's clothes into a closet, and told her to get out. Eva was scared."

CHAPTER 24

Old Friends

The breeze cooled Jennie's tear-stained cheeks as she walked through the trees along the Delaware River and up the hill. Shep tagged along, as usual. She anticipated the coolness and seclusion of the timber. It was the perfect place to think and be alone. Jennie hoped that Nate was working out in the field or fixing his dinner.

She sat up against a tree that leaned north, the result of fighting many years with strong, southerly winds. *What makes him think he has the right to tell me what to do?* she thought angrily, then shook her head, reminding herself she should calm down and not get wound up again.

Jennie hated that her father could make her feel this horrible. Her mother was right; she wore her emotions for all to see. She supposed this was at the heart of what got her into trouble in Kansas City, along with the fact that she could be so reactive.

She tried to relax and take things without worry, but it went against every part of her. It was the excuse she now used for relying on alcohol to calm her. Besides being illegal in 1923, drinking was not something she enjoyed. Having a relationship with Hunt, however, meant nights spent at the speakeasy. It was perhaps the only thing she regretted about the lifestyle he gave her. She thoroughly enjoyed being treated like a lady instead of a servant, which was how she sensed life would be if she married someone like Lon Myers. There certainly wouldn't be any symphonies or art galleries in her future. Only a wind-up Victrola and some 78 records.

Jennie had the ability to carry herself well and fit in with the country club crowd, when needed. Hunt didn't seem to mind that he was unsure who his real friends were. He knew how to play the game and use everyone as much as they used him. Did Hunt really know who Jennie was? No matter. He liked the woman she was pretending to be.

Lately, Jennie wasn't feeling like herself. Every little thing set her off, launching her into a tirade. She struggled to control her temper. So many conversations turned into arguments, which usually ended in tears. It took hours to fall asleep at night. She hated the thoughts that invaded her mind at that hour, when she could do little about it. If only she had the farmhouse to herself, there would be peace and quiet. If only they were gone, things would be all right. *But no!* she cried out in her mind. *I cannot think of such things.*

If only God would take me to heaven. That would be such sweet sleep. She remembered that Lon's wife had shot herself, but wondered if that were really the case. How could a woman put the barrel of a rifle to her temple and reach all the way down to the trigger? She pondered this for a long time. She looked at her arms. They were pretty short.

The last tear of anger and confusion spilled onto her apron. She squinted to see a cluster of dogtooth violets suddenly appear in front of her. She knew the hand offering them must belong to her childhood friend.

"Home is not the same, eh?" Nate said softly, supposing yet another run-in with her father.

"No, it's not." She pulled a handkerchief from her pocket and wiped her nose. "But neither am I."

"You haven't changed much. I still know where to find you." He smiled.

She laughed a little. "I guess so. But I'm not the same girl you led out into the timber, years ago."

"You've changed?"

"It's more how things around me have changed. For one, I don't want to live on the farm with that woman."

"Who?"

"Holly. Ernest's girlfriend. It's only a matter of time before they're married. What will happen then? Will they force me out of the only home I've ever known?" She gently touched the edge of the flowers. "Nate, I don't like who I am when I'm here. I don't like living with an old man who thinks his last job on earth is to make sure I marry someone he approves of."

"Is Eva still at the farm?"

"No. She got a job in Meriden as a housekeeper. It's really for the best. She needed to get away before they made her into another servant."

"Maybe your father's only trying to make sure you'll be taken care of, once he's gone."

"I'd be happy if they just left me alone on the farm."

"Wouldn't you be lonely?"

"I have friends in Kansas City. They'd come visit. We have so much room, I could invite half the town at the same time."

"Maybe that's what he's afraid of. Besides, it doesn't look right for a beautiful woman to live alone."

"There's plenty of old maids in Meriden and Perry."

"That's different. No one will have them."

"And I won't have anyone around here, either."

He knew she was right, but it cut him to the bone. She would never have Nate. He simply didn't have enough to please her.

"That sounded awful," she admitted. "I'm sorry."

"Word is, Ernest will get the farm when your dad dies," Nate said.

"I'm not surprised. But I'm the one he owes."

He raised his eyebrows, questioning.

"We both signed a contract three years ago. Dad agreed to pay me seven hundred dollars a year to take care of the house. Still haven't seen any of that. He also was going to give me half of the chicken and egg money."

"That's quite a lot," Nate commented.

"It's about twenty-five hundred dollars at this point. Enough for me to get out of here and start over, somewhere else. If things don't change, I'll only be here as long as it takes to get my money back."

"You wouldn't have anyone to care for you."

"But I do, Nate," she admitted. "And he's going to give me the diamond ring I've always wanted."

"Lon agreed to that?"

"No. Someone else. Can't say who, just now. Let's just say that things are not as they appear."

"What do you mean?"

"How would you feel if I married somebody you didn't know?"

"Not Lon?"

"Let's just say I'm waiting to see how everything comes together."

"So you don't want Holly to live at the farm?" he prodded.

"No," she answered coolly. "Definitely not."

"Harvey Barry told me you said that if you couldn't live there, no woman could."

"That's right. That's exactly what I said."

"Jennie, please don't do anything rash."

"You know me better than that, Nate. I just need time to think."

CHAPTER 25

Final Wishes

1922

Last Will and Testament of T.A. Hurley:

In the name of God, Amen:

I, T.A. Hurley, of Meriden, Kansas, being of sound mind and disposing memory and realizing the uncertainty of human life and certainty of death, do hereby make, publish, and declare this to be my last will and testament, hereby revoking any and all former wills by me made.

Direct the payment of all my just debts.

I give and bequeath to my sons/daughters the sum of $25.00 and no more of my property.

I am indebted to my daughter, Jennie Hurley, in the sum of $1,000.00, and in addition to said specific legal act bequeathed to her, I do hereby bequeath....

My son, Ernest R. Hurley, is now 26 years of age. He has remained on the homestead with me all of his life, devoting all of this time to the care of his invalid mother during her lifetime and to the full management of my affairs and the homestead.

He has done this to the sacrifice of an education and in order to stay and care for me in my old age, and manage and operate the homestead.

For the faithful devotion of my son, Ernest R. Hurley, to his mother and to me during our declining years, it is my desire and I therefore give, bequeath and devise all the remainder of my real and personal property to be his property absolutely subject only to the payment of the debt due my daughter Jennie, above mentioned, and the payment of all my debts owing at the time of my decease and all of my funeral expenses.

Signed, Thos. A. Hurley

On the same day, a warranty deed was executed and delivered to Ernest, for all of Thomas' real estate, subject to a mortgage against the property for $3,000, which Ernest would assume. Ernest was named executor of Thomas' will.

Ernest Ray Hurley and Helen "Holly" Cook were married on Good Friday, the 30th of March, 1923. This happened despite the warning of Holly's father. He advised her not to marry into the Hurley family. "They're a bunch of fighters," Mr. Cook warned.

The new couple planned to make their home after June 1 at Royal Hills House in Meriden. Until then, Ernest stayed at the farm with Jennie and Thomas. On Fridays, Ernest made the long trip over to Florence in the family's Ford, more than a hundred miles southwest, where Helen taught school. He brought her back to the Hurley farm on weekends.

Jennie pulled the reins back on her horse, Penny, as she rode up to the barn. She'd come from teaching a piano lesson over in Olive Branch Township. Thomas sat waiting on the wood box, ready to put the horse and buggy away.

"Your visitor is still here," Thomas said. F.A. Sheldon was a Union Pacific Railroad engineer that Jennie had met when she taught school in Omaha. He'd hired a carman to drive him out to the farm, the night before.

"Dad, about that money," she started.

"I've already told you, you'll get it!"

"But why are you making me wait until you die?"

"Jennie, I don't have that kind of money laying around. Even if I did, I wouldn't give it to you. You need to settle down with Lon. He knows how to manage money well."

"He'll just plow it back into his farm."

"That's fine. Probably the best place for it. I certainly don't want it spent on fancy clothes or new cars."

"You don't trust me! Well, it is my money, isn't it? There's no reason why I shouldn't be able to spend it on whatever I please."

"This is the only way I can be sure you'll be cared for."

"Dad, I will marry Lon," she said emphatically. "I've bought the wedding dress. Maggie and I are addressing the invitations. What else needs to happen so you'll believe me?"

"When I see you walk down the aisle. You've got a bunch of mail again." Thomas slapped a pile of envelopes on the table. Letters came for Jennie every day with return addresses bearing unfamiliar names. Many were from Kansas City.

"They shouldn't be writing to you anymore. It's not right, now that you're getting married," he asserted.

"I'll tell them, Dad."

"Does that fella inside know you're engaged?"

"Of course. I told you, he's just a friend."

Mr. Sheldon did think Jennie was engaged—but to him. She promised to tell her father "at just the right time," she said. His failing heart wouldn't be able to take the news that she'd be moving so far away, she told Mr. Sheldon. Her brother would be so excited about the impending marriage that he wouldn't be able to keep it a secret. So the railroader came and went without expressing his intentions to either man. Jennie's plans were becoming a reality.

When a box of candy and flowers arrived for her a day or two later, Thomas told Lon about the man's visit. "He seemed pretty taken with her."

Jennie overheard the conversation. "Dad, why don't you go out and sit on the back porch so Lon and I can talk about the wedding?" She helped him up from his chair.

"Certainly," he replied without hesitation, glad she was finally showing an interest in the marriage. "I'd hate to get in the way of you two lovebirds."

"Lon," Jennie began, "that man who came, he's just a dear friend who knows it wouldn't be right for us to carry on our friendship once we're married. His visit and presents were a way of saying goodbye," she explained.

"I see."

"That's all right with you?"

"No harm in someone giving you his best wishes."

"Good. Now let's talk about the wedding." She sat next to him, smoothing a crease in the tablecloth. "We both know we're not a couple of kids. Not like Ernest and Holly, who are just starting out. We've both acquired some material goods, and have some financial means."

She paused, considering the best way to broach the subject. "We're both much older. You've been married before, Lon, and I've had a life of my own in the city. In some ways, I guess you could say we expect more from marriage, but also less."

"What do you mean?"

"Well, we don't have all those silly romantic notions," she said waving her hand, "and we're more stable. Financially, that is." She looked up at him through long, dark eyelashes. He nodded. "Another thing. I'm accustomed to living more comfortably than most young women. Especially women who live around here. Wouldn't you agree?"

He nodded.

"Now, you know I've not had an easy life since I came back to the farm. Dad owes me a lot of egg money, and what I loaned him to add onto the house. But that money won't come my way until he dies, heaven forbid. Even then, it could take months to sort out the estate. The will is solid, but it will take time, you see."

He nodded again, unsure of where this was going.

"Once I get that money—it is a lot—I can afford to buy some nicer things I'd like to have. In the meantime, I'll be needing some new clothes. It's been almost ten years since I worked a steady job, and that's how old my clothes are. Frankly, I'm downright embarrassed to wear them, they're so thread-worn. I can barely repair what needs mending."

He actually felt sorry for her. "Won't your father give you a little something? How about your piano lesson money?"

"That doesn't begin to cover what I need. That's just my 'mad money.' Dad doesn't understand. He's still wearing the same suit he wore when sister Kate got married. Besides, every woman needs a new trousseau when she marries. It's tradition."

Lon scratched his chin. "A trousseau?"

"My going-away dress. A pretty new nightgown and robe. And some undergarments. What a lady typically needs when she gets married."

"I can't recall my first wife having that, but you're more aware of those things. Tell you what. I'll be glad to buy that for you, as soon as we're married."

"But not before then?" she said, her eyes wide.

"Well, maybe just the dress."

"Oh, you're so kind," she said sarcastically. "And of course, that includes the ring." She looked up at him. He sighed, wondering how much that would cost. "It doesn't have to be fancy, but I'll have it for so long that we really should make sure it's nice enough so we won't have to replace it, on down the road."

"How much are we talking?" he asked bluntly.

"I don't know any figures. Let's just say something as big around as the end of my little finger. Like this," she showed him.

"How much?" he asked.

"Maybe somewhere around a thousand dollars."

He gasped.

"Well, maybe not that much. We'll just have to go to Kansas City and look. Besides, it really is an investment."

Lon sat back in his chair and folded his arms. "We'll go ring shopping this weekend, but it won't be Kansas City. We'll go to Topeka."

"But they won't have anything worth looking at," she protested.

"I bought my first wife's ring there. Suited her just fine."

"Now Lon, I've talked to Maggie, and she says Ben really wished he'd gone to Kansas City and bought something nice when they got married, instead of buying her something bigger, later."

"Jennie, I'll be honest with you. I don't have that kind of money laying around."

"Sure you do; you're one of the biggest farmers around."

"Maybe, but I don't keep that kind of cash on hand. I've got it all tied up in the farm. If I had it to spare, I'd buy more cattle." He could tell she was irritated. "Look, I want to give you a nice ring but that's just too much money."

She got up and left the room.

"Where you going?" Lon called. "What in the world am I getting myself into?" he whispered to himself.

In a moment she reappeared, holding a pink satin bag almost as big as her hand. "I really didn't want to do this, but you give me no choice." She stood at the piano and opened the bag. Several diamond rings spilled out.

"Look," she said, pushing them around with her fingers. "You're not the first man who's wanted to marry me. These are from others who thought they could keep me. As you can see, I'm not easily pleased. You're going to have to work a little harder."

Lon was stunned by her sudden greed.

"Would it make any sense for me to marry someone who could only give me more of what I already have, maybe even less?"

"So, other fellas gave you these rings?"

"You catch on fast! I told you, I'm not a naive girl who's lived her whole life out in the middle of nowhere. I've lived an entire life away from here that you can only imagine."

He swallowed hard.

"It wouldn't be such a big deal, except that I've always wanted a diamond as big around as my little finger. I'd buy it myself, but as I said before, I won't get that kind of money until Dad dies." She looked at him, trying to figure out if he was convinced. To close the deal she said: "You'd be getting one of the most beautiful and desirable women in all of Jefferson County. Isn't that worth something?"

"Yes, but... that's a lot of money, Jennie."

"Okay, Lon. You think about it. And let's go ring shopping next weekend. By the way, while we're there, let's see about hiring a pilot to fly us from your farm to Kansas City, after the wedding."

Lon looked puzzled. "Whatever for?"

"We're planning to honeymoon at the Savoy Hotel, aren't we? Then we have to make a grand arrival!"

By the weekend, Jennie's mood soured. Lon sent word that he wasn't taking her to Kansas City. Ernest brought Holly home to stay, and Jennie stayed in her bedroom. Nate came over to play checkers with Ernest. Jennie came out long enough to eat and give him a present that one of her piano students made her. "Something to brighten your cabin," she said, her only pleasant words that evening.

As she walked down the hall upstairs, she kicked at Holly's trunk. The young woman's things were all over the house: her dishes, her clothes, and all the wedding presents she and Ernest had received. Their physical presence was like a slap in Jennie's face. It wouldn't be long before summer came, and then her new sister-in-law would be moving in.

"Where you going?" Thomas called as she headed out the front door with a large box.

"Lon's."

"What for?"

"To return his dishes. I made arrangements to get a new set."

"From Kansas City, I suppose."

"Yes," she said, kicking the door loudly. The pocket of her dress caught on the screen door handle. She cursed and fought with it, trying not to drop the dishes. "Why is everything so difficult these days!" she exclaimed.

CHAPTER 26

Frozen to the Bone

May 14, 1923

A steady rainstorm mixed with sleet fell that day. The wind was blowing stiffly from the north. The sky was gray, the air plain cold. All the roads got muddy, then started freezing. Only a strong team of horses could get through. Anyone who owned a car didn't dare get off the paved roads.

In the valley, the farmhouse lay silent. The hill to the north, covered by a large grove of trees, protected the farm. It was miles away from a highway, a half-mile from any neighbor.

In the afternoon Ernest talked to Ed Reed, one of the neighbors. As darkness began to fall over the countryside Herbert Judge, a nearby farmer, passed the Hurley farm. He saw Ernest driving the cows in from the pasture, whistling a merry tune.

As Reed rode back home, he was startled by a loud explosion. He turned to see where the noise was coming from. The Hurley farm was a quarter- to a half-mile away. He headed in that direction. As he got closer, he saw a wall of flames shooting through the entire house, and out the windows. The explosion had blown out the glass.

Reed pulled his team over to a fence and quickly tied them to it. He tried running across a freshly plowed field and a pasture to reach the house but his feet sank deep in the soggy ground. Almost five minutes passed before he was successful.

He could see the house burning outside, in a couple of places. *Is anyone home?* he wondered. *Are the Hurleys inside?* He went to the only entrance not consumed by fire: the back door. It was locked. Farmers usually left their doors unlocked in these parts, day and night, so this was unusual.

He ran around the house, trying to figure out what to do next. For a moment he watched the flames dance, then ran out to the barn, calling for Ernest. Then he hollered for Thomas, hoping to find one of them inside. No one answered. The only sound came from the cows mooing in the barnyard as they tried to back away from the radiating heat and firelight. Reed was beside himself; he didn't know what to do.

Shortly after, other people began to arrive. The blast had shaken their homes. One woman reported it was so powerful that her rocking chair started rocking by itself. Unsure where the loud noise originated, most neighbors simply followed the eerie glow up in the sky.

"What did you see?" onlookers questioned Reed, once word got out that he had been the first to arrive.

"What happened? How did it happen? Was anyone inside? What caused the explosion?" Their questions went on endlessly. Reed could only speculate and tell them he was close by, when the explosion occurred.

The heat was so intense that the crowd had to stay back at least fifty feet. Some began to fear the Hurleys were inside. Frank Sayles, who came with a neighbor boy, climbed the big tree in the front yard and watched the fire rage through an upstairs window.

By 6:30 p.m., the house had burned to the ground. Nearly one hundred farmers were milling around the scene excitedly. Since the entire house was engulfed, they made no attempt to put out the fire. "Has anyone called the authorities?" someone asked.

Then something odd happened. As flames reached the ground, they began to lick out across the icy soil, zigzagging back and forth in a trail less than two feet wide and as long as seventy-five feet. The people watched in amazement. "What caused it?" they wanted to know. "Where's it leading?" Within a few minutes the fire had reached a large barrel sitting on a wood frame.

"Look out! There's gasoline in there!" someone cried out. The crowd backed away just before it exploded and threw fragments everywhere. Fortunately, no one was hurt as the burning debris flew through the air.

"The flames must have followed a trail of spilled gasoline," someone supposed. "How could it have spilled unless someone

Genevieve “Jennie” Hurley toward the end of her life, holding a rose. Hurley Family photo

carried gas to the house?" The group theorized the fire might not have been an accident. "Did someone soak the house with gasoline and set it on fire?"

By 10 p.m., the red embers glowed eerily. Any hopes that the Hurleys were away for the night faded. In the half-light, three spirals of smoke curled up from different parts of the ruins. The sight of this made strong men shiver, realizing it was likely the place where bodies were located. The wind continued to blow from the north. Those standing on the south side of the house smelled something like burning lard. All but sure this pointed to death, the closest neighbors went back to their homes and called the authorities.

Tim Donovan, a detective with the Topeka police force and also a deputy sheriff, Dr. Marks the coroner, and Mr. Peebler of the funeral home in Topeka arrived by midnight. The ruins cooled sufficiently that they thought they could begin to investigate. Nearly everyone living within a five-mile radius was there. Hundreds of people were still standing around. However, by this time they had broken up into small groups, talking about the horrible event in hushed voices. Donovan and the other men were able to venture only a few feet into the remains of the house, since it was still quite hot.

"Maybe we should find something to drag over the ruins," the coroner suggested. They improvised and made grappling hooks by nailing long spikes into some boards, then doubling the nails over. Gene Cook's father, who was third on the scene, tied the hooks to a tractor and pulled out half-burned timbers and other debris. Three spirals of smoke continued to rise upward.

Once the debris was removed, the crowd gasped. The remains of three bodies were uncovered. The first appeared to be Thomas, who was lying on the north side of the house. Since the wind had blown the flames southward, enough of his body was left to make it identifiable. Apparently, the investigators surmised, he had been sleeping or lying on a cot when he died.

The second body was taken from the area where the kitchen

had been. The third came from the parlor, with a mattress on top. Only their torsos remained. It was impossible to tell each one from the other, although the overall snaps embedded in the flesh of the second body convinced them it was Ernest.

Once the bodies were recovered, the authorities began their most difficult work: determining what caused the explosion and deaths. The bodies were loaded into Peebler's car and taken to the funeral home. Peebler had anticipated the current road conditions by putting chains on his tires, yet his powerful vehicle barely made it through the mud. All the others at the scene had walked, or traveled by lumber wagons and horseback.

Deciding that nothing more could be done that night, the coroner and detective rode back to Topeka. The crowd thinned. A few remained on scene, talking and poking through the ruins, unwittingly destroying possible evidence.

CHAPTER 27

The Aftermath

By questioning those who returned to the farm the next morning, the detective and coroner learned about the fire that licked across the ground, to the gas tank. "It was apparent that the house was saturated with fluid, and this caused the flames to spread rapidly," Det. Donovan noted. *But why would anyone want to destroy the Hurleys and their home?* he wondered. *Were they all murdered by someone who set a fire to cover up a crime?*

The explosion was violent. How could gasoline poured in the house cause such a fireball and explosion? Some believed a power oil lighting system used in the house may have exploded, throwing fuel over everything. The detective clung to the notion that someone must have lugged bucket after bucket from the gas barrel to the house. Hurrying, they spilled much of it on the ground. The coroner agreed.

When they questioned the neighbors, no one knew why someone might want the Hurleys dead. "The three lived together in perfect contentment," one reported.

"Genevieve was a talented woman, a college graduate and expert musician. She taught school for several years in many different cities," another told the men. "She came home to her father's house last spring, to stay."

"Ernest recently married and intended to move away," yet another reported.

The detective and coroner went back to Peebler's undertaking parlor to examine the bodies. They made a discovery: part of Thomas Hurley's head remained. Attached to it were a few strands of hair, matted with blood. Examining closer, they found the back of his head had been blown off, presumably by a shotgun.

The sight of the two other charred torsos nauseated the detective. It was impossible to learn anything by examining them. They were so disfigured that no one could positively say whether they were human. All that remained of what was supposedly Genevieve's body was a blistered midriff. The detective surmised it could be something else—even the stomach of a calf.

Two young boys, Elmer Becker and Dick Christy, rode their horses over to the Hurley farm. With sticks they poked around in the ashes and found what appeared to be the bones of a dog.

The investigators discovered caked blood in the kitchen, where the remains of Ernest were found. The evidence was where Ernest's head would have lain. They determined that Ernest, too, had met with foul play before the fire. They did not find any blood near the spot where they found the body that supposedly belonged to Genevieve.

Herbert Judge, the Hurley's neighbor, was only able to tell investigators what he had told those first at the scene who gathered the night before. "We're up against a blank wall," Det. Donovan admitted.

"Maybe someone murdered all three, soaked the house with gasoline and burned it to destroy the evidence," Dr. Marks supposed.

"Maybe they had a terrible quarrel after the cows were driven in. One of them killed the other two, soaked the house with gas, then perished when the match was lit."

"Maybe it was accidental."

"How do you explain the gasoline, then?"

"You're right," Marks conceded.

"They had no known enemies, so that disqualifies the first conclusion."

"That leaves the second explanation."

"Double murder and suicide?"

"But who did it? Certainly not the old man. He was too old and feeble."

"Doesn't seem like Ernest would do it. Scarcely had time to, in the hour between Judge seeing him, and the explosion," Donovan concluded.

"No. Either it was a long, drawn-out premeditated deed, or it was the result of a sudden fit of rage."

"Perhaps Genevieve got jealous because her father intended to give Ernest several thousand dollars when he married."

"Think she planned a scheme to thwart his plans?"

"The old man seldom worked outside anymore, according to neighbors, so it would've been easy for Genevieve to take a shotgun and kill her father while he slept that afternoon."

"Then when Ernest came in, she could have shot him from behind. Maybe as he ate his supper, or even as he came in the door."

"To cover up her crime, she could have soaked the house with gasoline, then lit a match."

"Did she intend to kill herself?"

"Who knows? Maybe she planned to run after starting the blaze, but the explosion and fire spread rapidly, making her a victim of her own scheme."

Although the newspapers reported that this was the official verdict, Det. Donovan didn't believe it was true. He couldn't explain what caused the explosion, and never reached a satisfactory conclusion.

However, he did believe that Genevieve escaped the fate of her brother and father, and that the third set of remains may have belonged to an animal or even another person. And here is why: on the third day after the fire, a small package arrived in the mail for Genevieve. Postmarked Des Moines, Iowa, it contained what appeared to be a diamond engagement ring. This is when the coroner and detective learned that Genevieve was engaged to marry Alonzo Myers, the 51-year-old farmer who lived ten miles away. Genevieve had known Lon for many years and had been seeing him regularly since she returned to the farm.

Together with Dr. Marks, Det. Donovan questioned Mr. Myers, who was obviously upset about the whole ordeal. "Why would she have done such a thing?" he asked.

"I don't know," Lon answered, shaking his head. "Last Sunday, she was over to my house and we talked about working on the garden out front. We were going to be married, you know, and she was moving in with me."

"What was the old man going to do, then?"

"Most likely would've been alone, since Ernest and Holly were planning to live in Meriden, but I told Genevieve that Thomas could come live with us."

"Did you know that a ring came in the mail for her this morning? A diamond ring?" Dr. Marks questioned. "We're not sure, but it could've been an engagement ring."

"No, no." Lon was visibly stunned. "As a matter of fact, the last time I went to see her, she insisted I buy her a very large ring."

"Did you?"

"It wasn't a question of money. I have it, but it's all in my land and livestock."

"So, what then?"

"I told her no, that a smaller one would work just fine. She wouldn't have it."

"How did she seem to you?"

"Angry. I figured she'd probably call off the wedding. But her father said she'd calm down and forget about it."

"Anything else you want to tell us?"

"Just about the ring coming in the mail. Before I left, she went to her bedroom and brought back a small purse. Opened it, and poured out several rings on the piano. They all had pretty big diamonds. She told me I wasn't the only man who wanted to marry her. Then I began to think there were other men in her life."

"Did you suspect this before?"

"Well, she's never married. For as good looking as she is, maybe? But I never dreamed there could be so many."

"What was your reaction to seeing all of those rings?" Dr. Marks asked.

"I wasn't pleased, but if she wanted to, I'd have gone ahead and married her. A man my age can't be too picky. I did care for her."

"What happened to your first wife, Mr. Myers?"

"She was very ill. Took her own life. Doctor thought it had to do with the change of life."

"Can you tell us more?" Det. Donovan asked.

"We were going to see the doctor in Topeka that morning. I went upstairs and found her in bed. She'd shot herself. Died a few hours later."

"That was about a decade ago, as I recall," Dr. Marks said.

"Yes," he affirmed.

"Mr. Myers, we heard that something strange happened at your place recently," Det. Donovan said.

"What's that?"

"Did you find your horse dead this morning?"

"I did," Myers answered.

"Do you have any explanation for this?"

"No. In fact, it's the healthiest horse I've ever owned."

"Keep in touch with us," Det. Donovan said, before leaving.

CHAPTER 28

Wonderings

There was no name on the ring box that came from Des Moines, but the detective and coroner traced it back to Mr. Sheldon. He called a neighbor to ask about Jennie when he read about the fire in his local newspaper. Indeed, Mr. Sheldon had sent Jennie the ring, and expected to come and claim her as his bride within two or three weeks. He knew nothing of her engagement to Lon Myers.

"So Genevieve promised to marry two men at the same time," Det. Donovan thought aloud, back at his office.

"How many more engagements do you suppose she had?" Dr. Marks quipped.

"From the number of rings she showed Myers, could've been a half dozen or more."

"If they were engagement rings, was she lined up to become a bigamist?"

"Maybe she murdered her father and brother to escape the mess."

"I wouldn't be surprised if they had a big quarrel."

"I don't think she died in that fire," Det. Donovan dared to say.

"Why not?" Dr. Marks asked, astonished by this conclusion.

"Where are all of those rings that Myers saw?"

The two went directly to the site of the tragedy and made a thorough examination. No rings could be found. "Fire wouldn't destroy them, so someone must have taken them away," Det. Donovan concluded.

"You don't think she escaped with them, and somehow managed to make it look like she'd burned to death with her father and brother?"

"I think anything is possible at this point."

"Myers said that when he was at the Hurley home before the

fire, he saw a loaded shotgun behind the kitchen door. Yet we found the barrel of that gun in the living room."

"Both charges had been shot."

"The heat from the fire could account for that."

Neither man could be certain of anything at this point, so tangled were the facts. They swam like molasses in their heads. Yet this was their business, and they would get to the bottom of it, if they could.

"I'm calling a jury," Dr. Marks announced.

CORONER'S RECORD

Holding inquest (x) days, at $3.00 per day, Venire for jury, 25 cents, Subpoenas witnesses, 25c. each subpoena, Mileage (x) miles, 10c each way, Administering (x) oaths, 10c. each, Transcribing evidence, (x) folios, 10c. per folio, Transmitting evidence to County Clerk, 25c., Order of burial, 25c., Adjournments, (x) days, 25c. each day, Miscellaneous fees.

Dr. G.W. Marks: "I have examined the bodies of Thos., Earnest (sp) and Genevieve Hurley but could not decide whether foul play had been done.

"I saw the bloodstained clothes of Thos. Hurley and the remains of a body, and I can say I believe they were dead when fire occurred. There would likely be no shot in charred bodies as lead melts at a comparatively low temperature."

State of Kansas, Jefferson County: "An inquisition holden on the Hurley Farm in Jefferson Co., Kansas, on the 15th day of May 1923 before me, G.W. Marks, Coroner of said County, on the bodies of Thos. Hurley, Earnest (sp) Hurley and Genevieve Hurley, thereby dead by the jurors whose names are hereunto attached and subscribed—

"The said Jurors upon their oath do say that the said Thos. Hurley, Earnest (sp) Hurley and Genevieve Hurley came to their death by causes unknown. In witness whereof we have hereunto signed our names as witnesses: Chas. Grause, H.A. Ploughe, Ire (sp) Baker, Fred Metzger, Albert Metzger and John Ferrell. Attest

G.W. Marks M.D., Coroner, Jefferson Co., Kansas. 15 day of May 1923."

The coroner's jury verdict resulted in a ruling of a double murder and suicide. Jury members said they believed Genevieve had killed her father and brother, and then herself. The remains were examined for any evidence of poison but were in such bad shape that little could be learned.

A post-mortem resulted in indecision. The doctor said there might have been slight traces of poisoning, but this was doubtful.

"Perhaps," Det. Donovan reasoned, "Genevieve tried to kill her father and brother by giving them each slight doses of poison in their food. Maybe she found this too slow and sped it up with a shotgun."

Another strange discovery was made, which supported this theory. Some of the chickens on the Hurley place turned up dead. Because of the events that occurred at the farm only days prior, they examined the chickens and found their deaths were, in fact, caused by poisoning. If poison had been placed in the food, and the scraps thrown out for the chickens to eat, that would explain the flock's demise.

Had Lon Myers' horse come anywhere near the house that day, it could have ingested enough poison to die, as well.

CHAPTER 29

Triple Tears

All of Meriden and Jefferson County had never witnessed such a funeral as the one held for the Hurley family members. Three closed caskets were carried into the Methodist Church, then placed near the altar. Charles Cook attended to his grieving daughter Holly, Ernest's young bride. She sat in front and sobbed aloud during most of the service. Eight of the Hurley children were there for the family funeral. The church was extremely crowded. Many who came were unable to get into the church. Three funeral auto cars sat out front during the service. Mr. Peebler, the undertaker from Topeka, was there with his assistant and brother Paul, who came from Wichita.

People drove from near and far to pay their respects, some out of morbid curiosity. It was reportedly a day never to be forgotten in the little town of Meriden. Andy, Thomas' eldest son, was so full of grief that he could not attend the funeral. Instead, he used his restless energy to plow a field near the farm that day. He also was on the lookout in case the killer or killers returned to the scene of the crime.

The Rev. C.L. Day, pastor of the Meriden church, read the scripture and opened the funeral services with prayer. The Rev. Thorne, pastor of the Perry and Thompsonville churches, deviated from the tradition of reading the obituary notices. Instead, he spoke of the deceased more intimately.

"Of Father Hurley," he began, "I speak only from hearsay. I called at the home to see him on occasion but he was temporarily absent, so that I did not have the pleasure of meeting him. I am told, however, that he was a loving father, respected by his many acquaintances, and that he was upright and honest in his dealings with his fellow men. His great age and increasing helplessness made him quite a homebody in recent years, and so the outside world saw little of him. Of him, I would say all that could be said of a loving father, an indefatigable worker, and a law-abiding citizen. Mr. Hurley had lived his allotted three score and ten years and more, and many are those who grieve his passing.

"I met Miss Genevieve L. Hurley shortly after becoming pastor of the Thompsonville church," the Rev. Thorne continued. "I found in her a capable, willing worker, with high and holy ideals. Her musical talent she was always ready to use in the service of the Lord, and many are those who have been entertained and helped by her beautiful singing. Miss Hurley had a class of high school girls in the Sunday school, to whom she gave conscientious service. The fact is that in every good work she gave herself fully and gladly. Her tragic end is a great shock to the people of the Thompsonville community and a great loss. We shall miss her.

"Ernest Ray Hurley was, like David, a young man after God's own heart. A year and a half ago he united with the church, where he had displayed deep spirituality and rendered efficient service. He was treasurer of the Sunday school. The speaker recalls two statements that Ernest made in a letter to him a few weeks ago. In speaking of his work in the church, he said, 'I am anxious to learn to do these things in a business-like manner.' Another statement was this: 'I love the church.' Both he and his sister were very liberal in their financial offerings, always ready to support the regular work of the Kingdom and to help any and every worthy cause. The death of Ernest is a great loss to the Thompsonville church, and a grievous shock to his numerous friends. He, too, will be sadly missed."

After the funeral, a mile-long cavalcade of family and close friends processed behind three hearses up the winding road to Meriden Cemetery, which sets on a rise overlooking the community and valley below. Fellow Masonic members gave Ernest a special burial service, in addition to the standard graveside service given by the pastors for all three as they were committed to their final resting places.

So was added another chapter in one of the saddest tragedies that ever happened in Jefferson County. The Hurleys had many friends who raised a deaf ear to any claim that one member of the family had slain the other two. They didn't know the cause of the deaths, yet would not agree that any of the victims could have been the perpetrator.

CHAPTER 30

Bad Word Travels

Western Union Telegram. For Quick Service Answer by Bearer. Pay No Charges to Messenger Unless Written in Ink on Delivery Sheet. Charges—.50.

Received at Commercial Nat'l. Bank Bldg., 14th & G Sts., N.W. Washington, D.C. Always Open.

1923 May 22 AM 11 29

GARY IND 22 1012A

MRS NELLIE PUGH

AN ANSWER 3948 31 ST MOUNT RAINIER MD

FIRE DESTROYED HOME FATHER ERNEST GENEVIEVE PERISHED BURIED LAST THURSDAY WILL.

Nellie handed the messenger fifty cents and slowly closed the door. She scanned it quickly, then read it over and over, slower each time, making sure she was reading correctly. *Daddy, yes,* she thought. *He has been in poor health. But what about Ernest and Jennie?*

The telegram dropped from her fingertips to the foyer carpet, overturning as it landed on the floor. She covered her mouth, looking down at it and thinking to herself, *No, this isn't happening. If I don't pick up the paper and look at it again, maybe I can throw it in the trash and it will have never happened.* She leaned down and picked up the yellow paper by the corners as if it were some crushed bug that needed disposing. She was extremely careful not to turn it back over, and placed it in the can by the back door. Then she washed her hands and started supper.

"How was your day, dear?" Earl kissed Nellie on the back of her neck as she stood at the sink, peeling potatoes.

"Oh, just fine." She smiled, but her eyes were glazed over.

"I can't wait until it gets warm enough for watermelon. Here, let me dump those for you." Earl reached into the sink and pulled out a handful of brown and white vegetable skins.

"That's fine. I'll do it," Nellie insisted.

"It's no problem." They stood there awkwardly, he with his hands full, she with an incredible look of dread that something was out of place.

"Let me," she insisted, as if trying to block his way to the back of the kitchen.

"Nellie," Earl laughed, "whatever are you doing?" She wouldn't let him pass. He couldn't understand this odd behavior, and his lighthearted mood suddenly turned. "Nellie, stop this foolishness!"

She covered her face with her hands and shuffled across the linoleum.

"What's this?" He lifted the yellow page that carefully lay on top of the morning newspaper and eggshells. They were remnants of their breakfast together that morning, when everything had been right with the world. She would remember it as their last normal time together.

"Oh my word!" he whispered quickly as he read.

"I tried to make it go away." Nellie was sobbing as he went to her.

"Honey," he said, wrapping his arms around her and resting his chin on top of her head. She snatched the telegram out of his hand and tried to throw it across the room. It landed on the breakfast table beside them.

"You don't understand. I don't want to see it. Don't want it to be true. It's got to be a mistake." She looked into his eyes, pleading for affirmation. All he gave was a sad, regretful smile that told her yes, it must be true.

Not long after the funeral, a neighbor who lived a mile from the Hurleys showed up at Det. Donovan's office and told him that late one night, perhaps two or three in the morning, he heard a car drive past, in the direction of the Hurley farm. This was before the fire. "For a car to be out at that hour of the night was rather unusual in our area," he pointed out.

"What was the weather like?"

"As I recall, it had been raining and was pretty muddy. The car sounded as if it was having a hard time pushing through. I laid there in bed and heard it chugging through the mud and thought, 'Why, it must be going to the Hurley place,' as only three or four more houses use that side road."

"Have you told anyone else about this?"

"No. I really didn't want to get involved at first. But then I thought about it and decided to tell someone, so that whoever did it—if there was somebody—didn't go unpunished."

Det. Donovan inquired of every farmer who lived along the road, asking if any had visitors at such a late hour. None did. He deduced that the car must have gone to the Hurleys.

"Excuse me, sir." A man peered into the detective's office.

"What can I do for you?"

"About that fire near Meriden."

"You mean the Hurleys?"

"Yes, well, I run a hotel in Meriden, and I thought you'd like to know that a stranger came into town on the evening train about a week before this happened."

"And?"

"He ate at the hotel, then asked how to get out to the Hurley place. I wasn't sure where it was, so I sent him to a garageman. He knew the way but didn't think a car could make it. So he took him out in a team and buggy."

The stranger who hired the garageman was later identified as Mr. Sheldon from Des Moines, but this still left the first visitor, the driver of the car, unaccounted for. No one could say for sure just how many men Genevieve had promised to marry. The mailman told the detective that she received much correspondence. Perhaps the names of those men were contained in her personal letters. However, they all burned in the fire.

Is Genevieve dead? the detective wondered to himself. *I think she was too smart of a lady to plan her own death. Maybe she schemed to make it look like she died, but really escaped. If she wanted to be free of her circumstances by committing suicide, she wouldn't have killed her father and brother. It's more likely that she would have killed them and destroyed the house if she truly wanted to make a getaway and leave no trace behind.*

"Heard the latest rumor?" the coroner called and asked the detective. "Just before the fire, a woman's body was stolen from a dissecting room at the KU Medical School in Kansas City."

The detective drove over to the school, an hour away from the Hurley farm, and questioned school officers.

"Yes, the body of a woman has mysteriously disappeared," a school official confirmed.

"Where was it taken from?"

"Cold storage. Kept there with a large number of other cadavers."

"Why do you have so many bodies around?"

"For students to study and experiment on, so they can learn about the human body. By dissecting one, they can see where everything is."

"When did this happen?"

"During the night, about two weeks ago. We discovered it the next morning but didn't do anything about it, since we had little to go on."

"Does anyone know about this except the administration?"

"We've tried to keep it quiet, but word has leaked to some professors and students."

"Do they have any theories?"

"Some say a rival medical school took it. Others think students stole it as a prank or to liven up a party, if you'll pardon the joke. You know how medical students can be."

"I can only imagine."

"We have to get the consent of a person before death, or from an immediate family member afterward, to take possession of a body and use it for experimentation. There is also the opinion that perhaps this woman's distant relatives—the one whose body was stolen—weren't happy that she was being used to further medical science. Perhaps they decided to retrieve it so she could rest in peace."

The detective immediately connected the strange disappearance with the Hurley case. How easy it would have been, he conjectured, for someone to place a stolen cadaver in the house, as a substitute for Genevieve Hurley's body. Little did they know that, at one point, she had lived not far from the university.

Jennie's property was accounted for, and valued. Mostly it consisted of a set of hand-painted dishes at Ross Gillully's apartment, some bearing the gold initial "G."

All that remained of the farm was auctioned off on June 26. Holly Cook was sued, along with half of the Hurley family, by her new in-laws. Maggie and other siblings were contesting the validity of Thomas' will. Holly's father, Charles, paid for the attorney's fees. She promised to repay him but, to her family's knowledge, never did.

Holly should have received some compensation since most of her belongings, minus a few things she'd taken to Florence, burned up in the fire. And then, she also had lost her new husband. However, the new in-laws who sued her were not pleased that such a latecomer to the family would gain so much. Because of the recent marriage and updated will, instead of receiving 1/11th of their father's estate, each of Thomas' adult children would only receive 1/11th of Jennie's part of the estate, as her legal survivors. Holly stood to receive all that remained, as Ernest's surviving spouse.

The public sale at the farm included everything left in the barn: a 9-year-old mare, a year-old bay, two black mares, a pair of black colts, a shorthorn bull, three roan cows, a bindlecow, a light roan, a red cow, a calf, three geese and almost sixty pigs.

Holly's father bought the Hurley's Ford motorcar for ten dollars. From out of the tool house, other items were sold: log chains, augers, hammers, scales, hoes, axes, a seed blower and tub, wrenches, saw oil, traps, levels and vises, nails, a square, cement, windows, shingles, a scythe and stretcher, a cider press and salt bricks.

Meats and fruits stored in the cave just southwest of the house were the most sought-after items, along with canned catsup, cherries, peaches, pears, berries, gooseberries, plums, juice, sausage, ham and bacon.

When the sale closed and everyone received their pay, each of Thomas' surviving children received less than thirty dollars.

On November 21, 1923, in the district court of Jefferson County, Kansas, it was ruled that the defendant Holly Cook Hurley would receive two-fifths of the net balance of all moneys belonging to Thomas' estate, and the remaining three-fifths would be divided among the eleven adult children. In other words, Holly would receive $1,533.53 as Ernest's wife, and the rest of the family would each get $209.11.

This, however, was deemed unsuitable by some of the family. Led by Maggie Hurley Bowlby, Tom, George and Will filed a lawsuit against Holly, her father, Andy, Eli, Libbie Beisecker, Nora Baker, Nellie Pugh, Noah Harding (a tenant on the Hurley property), and W.T. King and Carl Berndt, administrators of Thomas' estate.

They alleged that Thomas' will was the result of the undue influence exercised upon his mind by Jennie and Ernest. That, at the time the new will was signed, Thomas was 85 years old, feeble in body and mind, and easily influenced. That he was afflicted at the time with heart disease and had been, for years. That Ernest and Jennie "wrongfully coaxed, persuaded and unduly influenced him to sign the will." That the other children, other than Maggie Bowlby, were not present when the will was signed, and knew nothing about its preparation or the terms thereof. That Thomas had great confidence in Jennie and Ernest, and relied upon their advice and judgment in all matters of importance, and his mind was subject to their will and control. That Jennie procured an attorney to write the will and Ernest paid the attorney to prepare it. That the will was unreasonable and unjust in its terms toward his children.

And that it was not Thomas' will, but the will of Ernest and Jennie, making it invalid.

Thomas had signed the new warranty deed, giving Ernest all of his real estate, and placed it along with his new will in a private box at the State Bank of Meriden. He told the banker that he was putting them there so he would have them under his control. Somehow, however, the deed was taken from the box, or lost. No one knew where it was until about two weeks before the fire and murders.

CHAPTER 31

The Ghost and Mrs. Darling

1926

Nora Darling, a longtime neighbor and close friend of Genevieve's, now living in Idaho, stood at a shop counter in Buhl, looking at merchandise. The bell rang on the front door and a woman entered. When Nora looked up, she couldn't believe her eyes. The woman reminded her so much of Genevieve Hurley. Nora looked down quickly, then up again as the lady made her way across the store. *It can't be,* Nora thought. *But what if it is?* She had to investigate more, to be sure. Nora tried to compose herself as she approached the lady. "Genevieve? Genevieve Hurley?" she questioned, as she got closer.

The woman let out a startled cry, quickly covered her face with her hands and fled from the store. Outside, she jumped into an automobile which sped away before Nora could see who was driving or note any details about the car. She stood frozen at the door of the store, unable to speak or move for a few moments. She didn't know what to do. Instead of notifying local law enforcement, she went home and wrote to her friends back in Kansas about what she'd seen. A week passed before the letter was received. By that time, no one in Buhl knew where the woman might be.

Word spread rapidly through the Meriden area that Nora Darling had seen Genevieve Hurley. Jefferson County residents were divided in their opinions. Det. Donovan heard of the incident several days after news reached the area but did nothing officially, since the case was closed. However, he believed Mrs. Darling's revelation fit nicely into his mental recreation of the events.

He later questioned Mrs. Darling when she came back to Kansas to visit. She recounted her story for him. In his opinion, since she had known Genevieve so intimately, he saw only a slight chance that she'd been mistaken. He believed her story. His conclusion?

"The truth may never be known, or it may be discovered with any passing day."

The Union Pacific's "Portland Rose" train traveled from Portland through Denver, and on to Kansas City. Nellie Hurley's husband Earl was riding the train on business and decided to stop at Meriden to see the three new graves. He saw a young man mowing at the cemetery.

"Could you help me find the Hurley graves?" he asked, as the lad shut down the mower. "I'm a member of the family. I married Nellie Hurley."

"Really? I'm Gene Cook. My half-sister Holly married Ernest."

"Guess we were kin for a short while, then."

"Yes. Awful thing, that fire. Ernest was one of my friends."

"I promised Nellie that I'd stop by. She probably won't come back. We live in Maryland, you see. The miles aren't the problem. Just might be too much for her to handle."

"I see."

"What do you think happened?"

"Not sure, but a fella named Nate Isaac told me something interesting."

"Really?"

"Said he sat on the hill next to his place and watched the farmhouse burn that night. Also said he'd rather see Jennie Hurley dead than to see her run away with some stranger who had a rubber-tired buggy."

Earl raised his eyebrows. "Wow, that's strange. What does Holly think?"

"She blames Jennie. Says Jennie told her, 'You can't take Ernest from us. He's been with us too long.'"

"Did you hear about the cake?" Earl asked. "Someone thinks Jennie fed Thomas and Ernest a poisoned cake, then dumped the leftovers in the chicken coop. They supposedly found all the chickens dead, after the fire."

Gene shook his head.

"What happened to Holly?"

"She married a railroader and moved to Arkansas City."

"Did they have any children?"

"A doctor told her she couldn't have any, so they adopted a baby. Next thing we knew, she was expecting. You heard about the lawsuit, I guess."

"Yes."

"Dad paid a lawyer for Holly since everything she owned burned up in the fire. All she had were the clothes on her back."

"I talked to Nora, my sister-in-law. She said Holly would've been satisfied with just one share of the estate, but your father insisted on getting all they could."

"I don't know anything about that," Gene said.

"We thought Jennie had to give up teaching and come home to take care of the men. Nora says otherwise. One of the granddaughters was on the farm when Jennie came back. Said she told Eva to get out, so she left."

"I did hear that."

"What about the lady who said she saw Jennie out in Idaho? What does your family think about that story?" Earl pressed.

"We heard that somebody spotted her in Chicago."

"Mrs. Darling knew Jennie well enough to recognize her. She gave piano lessons to the Darling children, was in their home many times. She didn't think Jennie could have done it, but must've had help. Then she had a wild idea about Jennie marrying some guy named Hunt that summer in Montana, and they're somewhere together."

Ten years later, Nate's brother Guy Isaac took Nate's Whippet car to Topeka. Nate had just paid him $30-50 for shucking corn—a summer's wage, according to Gene Cook. When Guy went missing, authorities found Nate's car in Topeka and Guy's body in Chicago. It was said that Guy favored his older brother. Whether this had anything to do with the Hurley tragedy was anyone's guess.

CHAPTER 32

Digging for Clues

1970

Lila was fond of Old Nate but still wondered about him when he'd grow cold, and close himself off from others. She told her daughter Chrisie about the time Jerry Charles found the little gun and Nate yelled at him. Both found it strange.

"Do you suppose Nate shot Jennie with the gun?" Chrisie blurted out.

"Surely not," Lila said. "He told me he loved her."

Lila became intrigued with the circumstances around Jennie's death and the fire, so she asked one of the Becker boys about it. He suggested she go to the Kansas State Historical Society in Topeka and read old newspaper accounts.

"Listen to this," Chrisie said, reading aloud. "A bit of caked blood and the fact that two shotguns were found in other than their usual places form the slight clues upon which Jefferson County officers are working in an effort to solve the mystery of the deaths of T.A. Hurley, 86, Ernest Hurley, 28, and Genevieve Hurley, 41, whose charred bodies were taken from the ruins of their home five miles southeast of Meriden, yesterday morning." The article appeared in the *Meriden Message* on May 18, four days after the tragedy.

"Oh my," Lila said, shaking her head.

"At about 7:30 p.m. Monday evening, fire was seen at the Hurley home by neighbors," Chrisie read on. "By the time aid reached there, the house was half-consumed. All the doors were locked and attempts to rescue the persons inside were fruitless.

"The body of the daughter was found in the ruins of the parlor. She usually slept in a room above the parlor, it was said. Near the body of the woman was found a shotgun with a cartridge in the chamber which had been exploded. Another shotgun was found beside the bed of the son. Alonzo Myers, fiance of Genevieve Hurley and a frequent visitor at the Hurley home declared, it is said, that he frequently had seen both guns behind the door of the kitchen."

"I didn't know they'd been shot," Lila exclaimed. "So someone did murder them."

"Sounds like it. Listen: 'Only the smoldering torsos of three persons were found, the remainder having been consumed by the flames. The body of the father was found to have a quantity of caked and clotted blood beneath the head, and marks on the bed clothing beneath him may have been made by blood.'

"The bodies of the two men had portions of their attire clinging to them when they were recovered, indicating that neither of them had actually undressed for bed when they had gone to their bedroom. The remains of the woman were so badly burned that it was impossible to ascertain as to whether or not she had predicted (died) before the fire attacked the body."

"How awful," Lila interjected.

"The father came to the United States from Cork, Ireland, when a lad of fourteen. He settled on the farm near Meriden in 1867. His wife died nine years ago. There were six sons and seven daughters in the Hurley family. The living of these are..." and then it tells their names and where they lived."

"What a large family," Lila commented. "You know, I don't think there was much love in the home where Old Nate grew up. I'll bet he wanted to be a part of that clan."

"You could get lost in a group that big. Now it talks about Jennie. 'Genevieve Hurley, who lost her life in the fire, had been a schoolteacher for seventeen years. For nine years, she had taught school in Jefferson County, and for eight years she was a teacher in the Kansas City schools. She quit her professional career when her mother died nine years ago, and with Ernest Hurley made a home for their father on the home farm.'"

Lila took copies of the newspaper home and studied them. It only made her think of more things to ask Nate. She visited him one day when Clay Alderson was at Nate's house to find out about Wolf Town. He also wanted to know about the old barn on his land, and a well that he'd dug.

"I noticed this path back of the brome field that leads down into the timber," Alderson observed. "Doesn't seem to go anywhere. Just circles back up to the top. You know anything about it?"

"Get out, get out!" Nate yelled, jumping up out of his chair and shaking his cane at him. "I don't want to talk anymore!"

Lila brought Nate more leftovers on her next visit. She didn't tell him she'd been researching the Hurley fire, or that she wanted to find out more about the woman he seemed especially fond of—the same woman who, by some accounts, was responsible for the deaths of her father and brother.

"Flew into an uncontrollable rage," one reporter supposed. Yet the idea seemed far-fetched to Lila. How could a woman overtake two men? What made her so angry?

"You said Jennie was pretty?" she asked Nate.

"Yes, she was a looker. Even the mailman would go by, hoping to see her unmentionables hanging on the line."

"Who was that?"

"Mike Koenitzer. He'd go home after his route and tease his wife Ann that he'd seen Jennie's pink undergarments hanging outside. She knew how to attract the men. Guess she did a lot of that in Kansas City, too."

"What did she do, there?"

"Taught school." A slight smile drew up on the corners of Nate's mouth. "She was like honey to the bee."

Lila was amazed by his openness and decided to take advantage of it. "You were attracted to her, weren't you?"

"A man would have to be a fool not to. Or dead. No, she was the only one I ever loved."

"I hate to ask, Nate, but you didn't kill her, did you?"

"Why on earth, because of the gun? You think I used that to...."

Lila shivered.

"You've been coming here all this time, thinking I might have killed someone."

"No. It's just that an unsolved murder... and you, acting like there was something to hide. Why else would a man punish himself by closing off the world, like you do?"

He sat in silence a while. Then he finally spoke. "Lila, when I lost Jennie, I lost everything. Nothing else mattered. Maybe she'd never marry me but I could still see her from time to time, whenever she came to visit. And then she moved back home. Why would I want that to end? And those two men? I worked right beside them for years. Nobody I respected more."

Lila looked down at the carpet, deep in thought. Then she looked up and met his gaze.

"Tell you what," he said. "Why don't you drive me out to the lake? I'll show you where she used to live. Maybe then you'll understand."

Not much was left of the old home place. A white fence stood on the south side of the road. Once they got out of the car and started walking around, Lila noticed parts of a limestone foundation peering up through the grass. As she kicked the dirt, she saw bits of white dishes, glass bottles and crock jars embedded in the ground. The mighty maple still stood vigil. South of there, a beach reached out to the waters of Perry Lake, lapping peacefully against the shore.

"Before diamond rings were so important to Jennie," Nate began, "we met up in the timber, over that hill, almost every day." He pointed to the west. "It was our special place. Then she moved away, and I didn't see her much. She came back in the summer and for holidays. But something changed."

"That must've been hard."

"You know, she didn't intend to marry Lon Myers. Her father arranged it all; she had something different in mind."

"I read where they were supposed to be married shortly after the fire. I also read something about a package arriving for her at the post office."

"Another poor soul she was stringing along. Had a hard time explaining that to Lon, as I recall."

"What did you think about Lon?"

"Good farmer. Lost his first wife and probably wanted to replace her. I tried to tell him it wouldn't work, but he wouldn't listen. Who knows? Maybe he had his sights on this land." He gestured south, across the lake. "But maybe he was like the rest of us, just smitten with her." Nate laughed. "Lon gave her two turkeys for her birthday that year. Named 'em Lon and Jennie. Pretty silly, huh?"

She smiled.

"Jennie didn't think so. Was expecting something more. Made her pretty upset."

"What about her father and brother?"

"They were good people. None of this should've happened." He stood with his hands in his pockets, shaking his head.

"What happened, Nate?"

"A car came to the house. Jennie told me it was some guy from Kansas City. He was going to take her away. She'd finally get that ring she wanted."

"Myers wouldn't give her one?"

"No. Thought he could change her mind."

"When was this fellow supposed to come get her?"

"Day after the fire," he said. "It's been a long time ago, but sure seems like yesterday."

"Tell me, Nate," she gently urged.

"It was raining, so I hadn't been out in the field. Rode down to the Hurley place, like always. When I got there, two buckets of milk were on the boardwalk. Shep was drinking from one of them. *Well, that's strange,* I thought. Walked up to the back porch. Jennie was lying there. Couldn't imagine what had happened. Saw blood on her apron. Then I thought: *Where are Thomas and Ernest?* Knew I had to go inside."

Lila felt a lump in her throat. She put a hand on Nate's arm to reassure him.

"Ernest was on the kitchen floor. He'd been shot. Went into the back bedroom. Mr. Hurley was on his cot. I didn't know what to do. So I went upstairs."

His voice began to crack. "When I went into Jennie's room, there was this man lying across her bed. He was shot, but still alive. I could tell he was in a lot of pain. So I went downstairs, grabbed the corn knife next to the fireplace. They used it to split kindling with. The handle had fallen off long ago." His voice trailed off.

"Was Jennie still alive?"

"When I got back to the porch, she was awake and kept apologizing. I knew she had something to do with it. But I had to take care of her."

"So, what then?"

"I threw the milk out of one bucket, filled it with gasoline, went back inside and poured it all around. Took a few trips. Made sure Jennie was safe. Carried her a safe distance. Shep kept following me, so I locked him inside."

He would say no more, except this: "You know, I'd rather see Jennie Hurley dead, than for her to run off with a complete stranger."

CHAPTER 33

As If It Were Yesterday

That night, Lila had a dream. She saw Jennie throw open the back door of the house and collapse on the porch, her hair falling around her. In her hand was a pistol.

"Jennie!" a deep voice called out. "Jennie!" Lila saw Nate run toward her.

"Oh Nate," she cried. "What have I done?"

There was a red splotch on her apron. "What happened?"

"Oh Nate, they're going to put me away forever."

"Give me the gun," he said. It was the same pistol Jerry Charles had pulled out of Old Nate's drawer, decades later. Jennie handed it to him, and he stuck it in his overalls.

"I just wanted to get away. I just wanted my money. I didn't want any of this to happen," Jennie said.

"Don't worry," he told her. "I'll take care of everything."

Nate went back in the house. When he came out he asked: "Did anyone else know about your visitor upstairs?"

"No."

"All right. Let's go."

"Where?"

"Somewhere far from here." He hoisted her up on his horse, and she cried out. "Nate, I've been shot."

"Meet me back at my cabin."

"One more thing: there's a body in the shed."

He looked at her, not sure what to think. Then he slapped the horse's hind quarter and ran back into the house. From a tin box hanging on the kitchen wall, he grabbed a handful of matches. He went outside and dumped one of the milk buckets.

After splashing gas all over inside, Nate went upstairs and noticed the stranger was holding onto something: the precious bag of gold dust that Mr. Hurley kept in the mantel clock.

He dragged the body downstairs and out the front door, then lifted it up onto the front seat of the stranger's car. In the shed he did find a second body. He dragged this into the house and laid it down in the parlor before dousing it with plenty of gas, to make sure it burned completely.

In her dream, Lila saw Nate light a match and heard a dog barking. Right after that, he locked the door and left. Then she saw a man behind the wheel of the car, and Nate pushing it into a creek. Bubbles came up from the water.

CHAPTER 34

Goodbye, Old Friend

That night, Nate also had a dream. His was much longer than Lila's, with more detail. It was a recurring dream. Sometimes he dreamed the whole thing. Other times, it came in bits and pieces.

There, in Nate's dimly lit cabin, Jennie closed her lovely brown eyes and stopped breathing. Nate held her lifeless body in his arms and sobbed like a boy. "I knew you would leave me," he whispered. "You could not have lived behind the cold iron bars of a prison cell. Now you are mine forever."

When soft morning light came through the cabin window, Nate wrapped Jennie in one of his mother's patchwork quilts. He made his way to the timber with a pick and shovel.

Though it was mid-May, the steady work caused Nate to sweat. Many times he stopped to mop his brow and lean on the shovel. His deep love for Jennie and the thought that he would one day lie close to her gave him great comfort. Just as the sun went down, he picked up his tools and headed to the cabin.

He had to remind himself that she was still dead. When he came in for supper he imagined she might be sitting up, waiting to eat with him. But there was no meal, no warm fire. Jennie's body lie motionless, wrapped in the same quilt he'd left her in.

Nate heated up some beans and sat there, remembering. He thought about their school days together. How he could always out-figure her, and how she always waited for him to walk to school. How he made sure she got home safely when the snow was deep. How they laughed and took their time on warm, spring days, and how she ran ahead of him that day to the secluded spot in the timber. And how he finally caught up with her, and she let him kiss her. *Now,* he thought, *I must finish the job.*

The moon was full. Without a lantern, Nate made his way to the barn. He harnessed Bill and Bob, his loyal work team, and hitched them to the buckboard wagon. He recalled how Jennie would wave at him as she drove by in her buggy on Sunday mornings, and how Shep would stop at his place, knowing she would soon return.

A whip-poor-will broke the silence, bringing Nate back to reality. Years of farming had left him with a strong back and arms. Now at 41, he could easily lift Jennie into the back of the buckboard. He spread one more blanket over her and climbed up onto the seat.

He made his way down the road, across the brome field, through the trees and down into the timber. The many trees standing close together made it impossible to ride all the way in, so he carefully laid Jennie on the extra blanket and pulled her the rest of the way. The full moon glowed through the treetops.

There, beside a new grave, he held Jennie one last time, whispering and softly humming, remembering the best spring evening they ever shared together. Even afterward, Nate knew she would never be his wife. Being a dear friend would have to suffice. And so, with one last tearful goodbye, he buried Jennie there, where the dogtooth violets bloomed. And the leaves were just beginning to unfold.

Part Three

CHAPTER 35

Banner of Honor

Routinely, Lila and Charles would bring Nate his mail, give him a shave and read the newspaper together. One day, they drove him over to the land he'd traded with them. They wanted to show him the progress on the construction of their new house, high up over the lake. As soon as the car stopped, Nate got out, headed north toward the timber and tripped on a wire. Charles took off running and helped him get up.

"Are there lots of squirrels in the timber?" Nate asked. "Are the whip-poor-wills calling yet?"

"Oh sure," Charles answered, focused more on the old man's physical well-being.

Later, back in Meriden, Nate told Lila and Charles that his eyesight was failing, and he could no longer drive his old blue pickup that had a dent in the side.

"I'll be going away for a while," Lila told him.

"What for?"

"Taking nurse's training so I can care for old people. Then when I'm done, I'll bring you over to live with us in our new house. Your sister is coming over to take care of you until I get back."

"I'll miss you, Lila."

"It won't be long."

"Promise me something. Don't ever sell the timber."

"All right, Nate."

"And when I die, just throw my body out there for the birds and squirrels to pick dry."

They played another round of checkers and read poems. Nate looked up from his game. "You know why they never found all those rings that Jennie showed Lon?"

"No, why?"

"They were just paste samples she got from the jeweler. She was trying to decide which one she wanted."

Lila thought for a moment. She supposed that was possible. "You know, Nate, you could do something nice with all the money the government gave you for your land. You've already done so much for us. Why don't you use it to help other people?"

"What do you have in mind?"

"You could put it into savings. Let the interest grow. Then use it to send a Meriden High School graduate to college. Maybe they could wear a white banner at graduation that said, 'Isaac Banner of Honor.'"

He beamed. He liked the idea.

When Lila left, she held his face in her hands. "Nate Isaac, I love you."

"Me, too," he said, unable to say those three little words.

During a break from nurse's training, Lila stopped by Nate's to visit him and his sister, Osey.

"I can't get him to eat," Osey confided in Lila. "His false teeth are missing."

"Nate, you know it's springtime, and all the leaves are beginning to unfold," Lila said.

"I suppose so," he said sadly.

"You know what we'll do, next time I come? We'll make that white banner of honor for the student who'll win your college money."

"Be a good nurse, Lila, and write my story," he told her. Then, turning to Osey he said, "She's going to write a story about me and Jennie. Lila, don't take time away from school if something should happen to me."

"Now, Nate," she said, "nothing's going to happen. You just stop talking that way, you hear?"

Lila got a phone call one day in 1971. It was from Osey. Old Nate had passed away on May 15, when the leaves had unfolded.

He'd gone outside early one morning, headed toward the road, fell into a ditch and died.

What a life, Lila thought. *Living all those years with love as just a faded memory.* She visited his grave and planted a rosebush near her old friend's headstone.

Months later, Lila ran into Andy Petesch at the hospital. He told her that when they moved the furniture out of Old Nate's house, they found a corn knife under his mattress. The blade had a permanent dark stain on it, probably from blood.

"Did you know anything about this?" he asked.

"Was it missing a handle?" Lila asked, remembering the story that Nate had told her, the day they were out at the Hurley place.

"Yes, as a matter of fact it was," Andy answered. "However did you know?"

Afterword

I came to this story because of my father. As a boy, he sat and listened underneath a dining room table as the grownups told stories. Why he never mentioned "the family fire" until I was in high school, I'll never know. When he finally did, he spoke about it as if it were an accident.

This is what Great-aunt Maggie wanted to believe.This is what he'd heard from others. The family thought the incident was caused by a lightning strike, or the oil-lighting system had exploded. They couldn't, simply wouldn't believe it was Aunt Jennie's fault.

One day, however, we learned there was something more to the story. Dad and I were coming home from Topeka after poring over old newspapers at the Kansas State Historical Society, across the street from the state capitol building. Only then did we start to make any connections. I still remember saying to him in the car on the way home, "Dad, I don't think this was an accident."

Decades later, I can still see him telling me how he remembered watching his dad, Grandpa Tom, wring his hands and ask himself over and over, "What the hell happened?" I am sure that losing three family members so suddenly and tragically, and in a way that led others to think his sister was responsible for it, had much to do with Grandpa's mental breakdown in 1938. Another factor was that he'd lived off the land in Colorado and only worried about his own needs for forty years. When he married my grandma, and two sons came along, suddenly there were bills and rent to keep up with. The Great Depression was in full swing.

At Dad's last class reunion, he was able to sit in almost every photo because he had attended most of Newton's grade schools. His family moved often. When his dad would get a better job with the railroad, they'd find a bigger house to move to. When he got cut off, which happened more than once, they'd move again. This went on until Grandpa could take no more. He lashed out at a coworker one day, and Grandma Helen agreed to have him committed to Larned State Hospital. These days, Grandpa Tom likely would've been put on medication and sent back home. In 1938, however, state mental hospitals were just getting started and had beds to fill. Grandma was left to figure out how to raise two boys alone.

Dad helped by working part-time jobs. Instead of playing in the high school band, which he greatly enjoyed, he sold concessions up in the bleachers. Often his mom baked cakes to make extra money. Downtown store owners allowed her to sell them out of their display cases. Even this was a challenge because sugar was rationed during World War II. You could only buy so much at a time, and the ration coupons were in short supply. Great-aunt Maggie sent money to help but wanted to review Grandma's grocery receipts. Maggie would write back, questioning the items she thought were unnecessary.

After my mom and dad married in 1947, Grandma Helen moved to Larned, where Grandpa had become a permanent resident. He was a trustee worker, caring for the most violent and criminally insane inmates. They never divorced, living in the same apartment or double room in their final years.

All of this affected my father deeply. So did the fact that his parents died within a few days of each other. His mother had a heart attack and was gone the next week. Hearing the news, Grandpa Tom simply waved at Dad and said "Bye-bye" from his hospital bed. His body was suffering from a recent fall and broken arm.

All of this happened before I came along. One Christmas Day when I was about 12, Dad made copies of old family photos and gave them to us kids. They were of Grandpa Tom and his family, and his life up in the mountains of Colorado. Some of them are in this book. They remain one of my most treasured Christmas gifts. I spent hours looking at each detail with Dad's magnifying glass.

And so, I believe I have done the same here, looking at all kinds of details. It has taken thirty years to tell this story. Once or twice along the way, I lost the entire manuscript and had to start over. At some point, I also wrote a screenplay.

I wish I could go back and see the Hurley homeplace as it was, when I first saw it around 1981. In recent years it has been covered over by cane, brush and trees, the result of yet another flood. It seems the Corps of Engineers project didn't fix everything, after all.

We first went to Perry Lake when Dad and I visited Great-aunt Libbie's son Lester, his wife Jane and daughter Beth. "Les" was eight years younger than Ernest, and remembered much. He showed us the remains of the foundation, where the house had been. Where a little bridge and cellar once were. Where they kept a flock of geese. Jane pointed up at a rooftop, on a hill to the west. She said the lady who lived there had taken care of the elderly in her home. I couldn't imagine such a thing. Later, I learned this was Lila's house. I would go there perhaps a decade later.

When I went to Washburn and KU, I was drawn back to the lake and the remains of the Hurley farm. I would lie on the picnic table under the branches of the big maple tree, a respite from noisy dorm life. My understanding was that the land was leased to the Menninger Foundation in Topeka so their employees could use it as a recreation area. However, I wondered: how many of them slept in tents at night, knowing this was the site of an unsolved tragedy?

And then one day, after I got married and became a new mom, the phone rang. My oldest son Gannon was sitting in the high chair, probably eating fish sticks and tater tots. It was Dad. He told me that Jane, Lester's wife, had called. She'd seen an article in *The Topeka Capitol-Journal* featuring a woman who'd written a short story about the Hurley fire. She was looking for someone to lengthen it into a book.

Soon after, I got ahold of the reporter, Phil Anderson. He led me to Lila. Within a week or so, Dad and I drove up to Lila and Charlie's house, known as The Lake Place. She came out and met us at the intersection close to her house. I can still remember seeing her pretty white teeth as she smiled. We got to know each other and agreed to work together. My goal was to expand the story so that readers would care about the people who lost their lives that night. I wanted them to become three-dimensional and not just victims of a horrible crime.

Over time, Lila and Charlie became like family. They invited us to spend the night. Charlie would grill us pork chops and make his special barbecue sauce. In the morning Lila would fix a bunch of buckwheat pancakes. Wild critters would come to the deck and enjoy the leftovers. The McCabes never stopped taking care of creatures in need. Chrisie, her husband John and I are the only ones who remain, besides the next generations of their family and my sons, Gannon and Dakota. Charlie and Lila were like grandparents to them, a true blessing.

One afternoon when I was at The Lake Place, Lila watched Gannon so I could go exploring. They were probably sitting on the floor playing checkers, or with the miniature barn and animals in the basement. I wanted to find my way down the hill, walking the remains of the road that once connected Nate's shack and Jennie's house. I could almost hear his horses' harnesses jingling.

Farther down, I stopped to bend over and tie my shoe. It felt as though someone were watching me. I looked up to see a whitetail deer running away.

I continued on, wading through waist-high thickets until I reached a rock jetty. Dark clouds hung low, and the wind was blowing. I pulled up the collar on my baggy leather coat and shoved my hands in the pockets. I had finally reached the western shore of Lake Perry. Here, I could look across the water and see where my grandpa and most of his siblings were born and raised. It was just as I imagined: things did look different, from this perspective.

Kim Hurley Andrews
May 2025
North Newton, Kansas

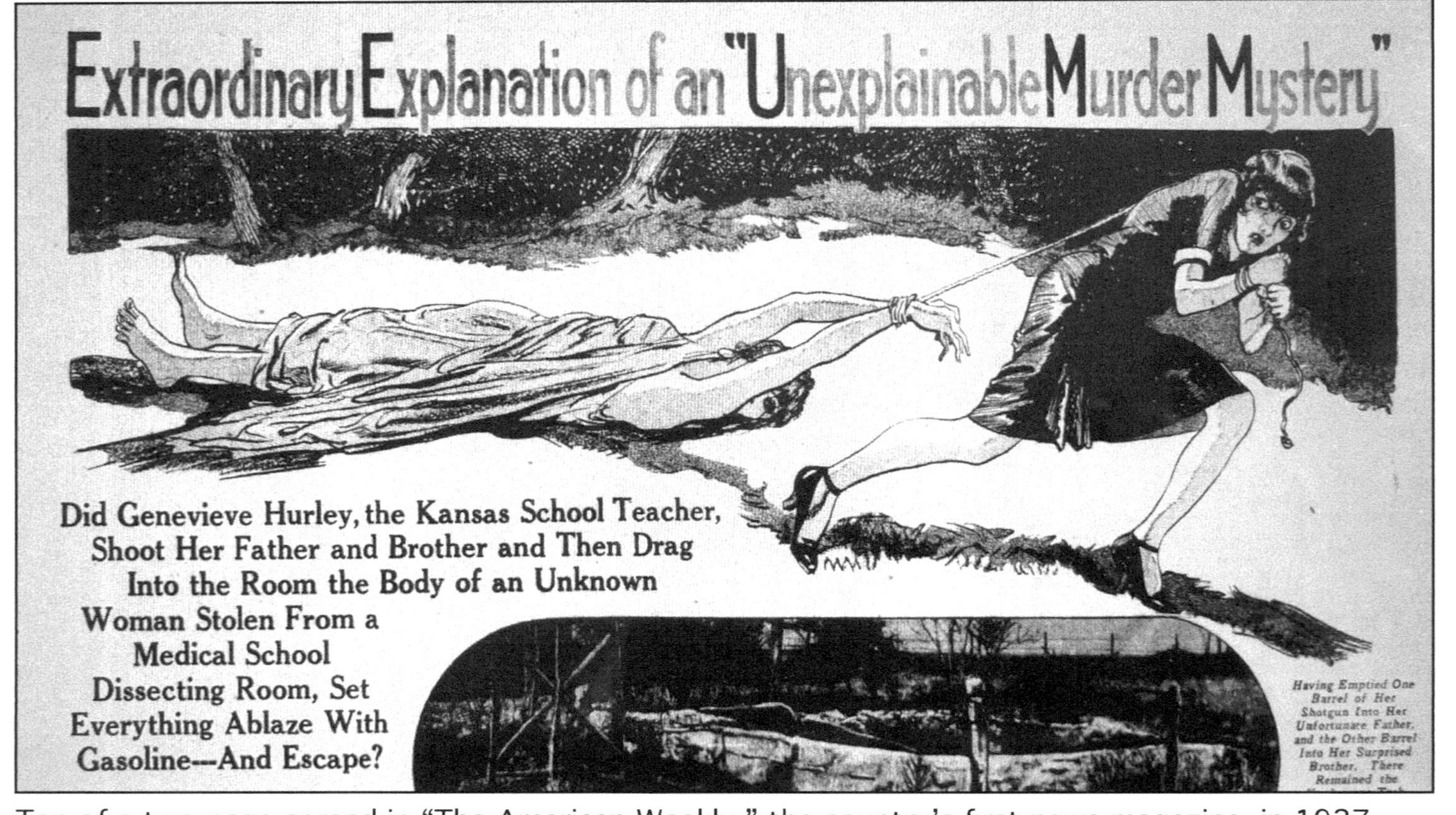

Extraordinary Explanation of an "Unexplainable Murder Mystery"

Did Genevieve Hurley, the Kansas School Teacher, Shoot Her Father and Brother and Then Drag Into the Room the Body of an Unknown Woman Stolen From a Medical School Dissecting Room, Set Everything Ablaze With Gasoline---And Escape?

Having Emptied One Barrel of Her Shotgun Into Her Unfortunate Father, and the Other Barrel Into Her Surprised Brother, There Remained the

Top of a two-page spread in "The American Weekly," the country's first news magazine, in 1927. Jennie Hurley is depicted as a flapper. Inserted into Sunday newspapers across the country.

The remains of the big maple tree out front of the farmhouse, ca. 1992. Kim Hurley Andrews

My dad, Lucius ("Mike") Metzger Hurley, standing next to Lila McCabe on the old Hurley homeplace. Perry Lake and Rock Creek bridge are in the background. Photo taken facing ESE, about 1992. Kim Hurley Andrews

Last night I dreamed in colors bright, orchid pink and blue.
You were there within my dreams, I swear to you it's true.
You rushed into my waiting arms; I held your body close,
And when you laid beside me was the part I liked the most.

A soft breeze moved the pink curtains, blue moon lit up your face.
And then you left this bed of mine and floated into space.
You went right through the wall somehow upon the moonlight's beam.
It broke my heart to watch you enter someone else's dream.
Dream girl, please come to me, so I can dream and dream and dream.

The days go slow, I hurry home, anxious for the night.
I wait for you to come to me in dreams and hold you tight.
Within whose dreams do you belong? Now many dreams you see.
I only know I want to sleep and dream you back to me.
Dream girl, please come to me, so I can dream and dream and dream.

—"Dream Girl," song by Delila Mize McCabe

Genevieve "Jennie" Hurley, Old Nate's "Dream Girl."
Hurley Family photo

The Grateful Woman

Now that you have read the story of Genevieve Hurley, her family, their lives and tragedy, I want to introduce you to another woman. Her story is one that has given me hope. It is the story that God used to call me into ministry, found in Luke chapter 7. I did not recall reading about her before, in such a profound way. When I finally did, it seemed as though I were right there, watching it all happen.

She appears, soon after Jesus runs into a funeral procession. A young man has died, and his mother is at the head of a procession to bury him. His body is being carried by other men on something called a funeral bier. Not beer that is drank, but a basket or woven material that they laid him on. Jesus, full of compassion—both for the young man who has died, and his mother—stops to meet them. (All women were dependent on men then, for their place in the world.) Somehow Jesus knows that the young man's mother is a widow. Now that he is gone, she is as much a goner. Her only choices as a woman without a husband and a son are to live with other family or hire herself out to someone else, as a servant or slave.

So Jesus, as we are shown in the Gospel of Luke, over and over, is a man whose heart is full of compassion. He doesn't know these people, has probably never met them and yet, stops in his tracks. (Does this tell us anything about how we should be, with people we've never met, if we are truly his followers?) Jesus stops the procession, puts out his hand, and brings the young man back to life. I can only imagine the astonishment of those carrying him. Do they drop him? One wonders. In a moment, two people's lives are revived. Restored. Not resurrected, however; only Jesus is the one this has happened to, at this point. When he returns, according to scripture, we all will be resurrected, our bodies from the graves, in a way we cannot explain or understand at this point.

After this, Jesus takes someone up on an invitation to eat at their house: a religious man who is curious about Jesus. So curious and distracted that he forgets, conveniently, to offer him basic signs of hospitality when he arrives. Perhaps he would only do this to people he deemed worthy to receive it. (Again, we can reflect on our own times of inaction, when we have withheld hospitality because we decided the people weren't important enough.)

Jesus is eating while he lies at a table with others, as they did in those days. Somehow a woman barges in, uninvited. She is *that* woman, known to all in the town or village as someone who has a reputation for being a sinner. She has done something or things so bad that whatever she has done has become her identity. Not only did she sin; she is a sinner. Perhaps we have been worried or even felt something similar, in our lives: that people have looked at us with only our worst moments in mind.

This woman comes to Jesus without a word, desiring to show her gratitude in some tangible, meaningful way. This is the place where I was gripped, and have been gripped for almost two decades. Without a word, she begins to weep at his feet. Not just a few silent tears, but so many that she can wash his feet with them. Her tears fall on his size 9's or 10's or whatever the common man's shoe size was, in Jesus' day. And we know his feet are dirty, because the host of this dinner party has not taken the time to properly wash them or tell his servant to. (Jesus points this out to the host, the minute the man starts ostracizing the woman for her outlandish affection.)

If this wasn't enough of a scene, the woman takes her long, unloosened hair—something offensive to those who thought it should be tied up on her head—and dries his feet with it. Did I mention she's also kissing his feet while this is going on? Not just once or twice, but over and over again.

Some may be repulsed by this. The host certainly was, but I wasn't. In fact, it mesmerized me. Who in the world would crash a private dinner party, so full of gratitude, go where they were not wanted, and let someone know how grateful they were? I wanted to know more. I had so many questions. It seemed as though I were standing there, watching it all happen.

In that moment, Jesus looks over and sees horror and chastisement on the face of his host. Jesus has something to say to him. He says, "You see this woman? She has done everything that you should've done for me, the minute I walked through your door. To the nth power, she is doing it. You did not give me a kiss of peace, which is a tradition for a host. You did not anoint my head with oil, another tradition of hospitality. She has poured precious perfumed ointment on my feet. You did not wash my feet. She is doing this, with her own tears.

"Do you want to know why this woman is so grateful, and why she loves me so much? Because she has allowed me to do much for her. To forgive her of much. Yes, she had much to be forgiven for. But now she has great love for me, as a result of letting it all go and giving it all to me.

"And Simon?" he asks the man by name. "You want to know why you love me little? Because you have let me do little, if next to nothing, for you. Either you don't think you have anything to forgive, or you just haven't realized it yet. Until you do, and sincerely ask for my forgiveness, you won't feel any love for me. At all."

This story is good news for all of us. Because the one who seemed so far from God was able to be reconciled to him, and also received a greater capacity to love him, as a result. We may find ourselves in the one who needed to receive forgiveness, and was extremely grateful to receive it... or in the one who was holding back and wouldn't acknowledge any need to be forgiven.

The good news of Jesus Christ is that God is able, through him, to bring reconciliation to both. All that's required is a heart open to being loved and forgiven. May your love for God, the Father, Son and Holy Spirit increase as you allow him to work in your life, more each day.

Be God's glory!
Rev. Kim Andrews

Thomas Hurley-Related Places in Jefferson County, Kansas
By Stan Funston

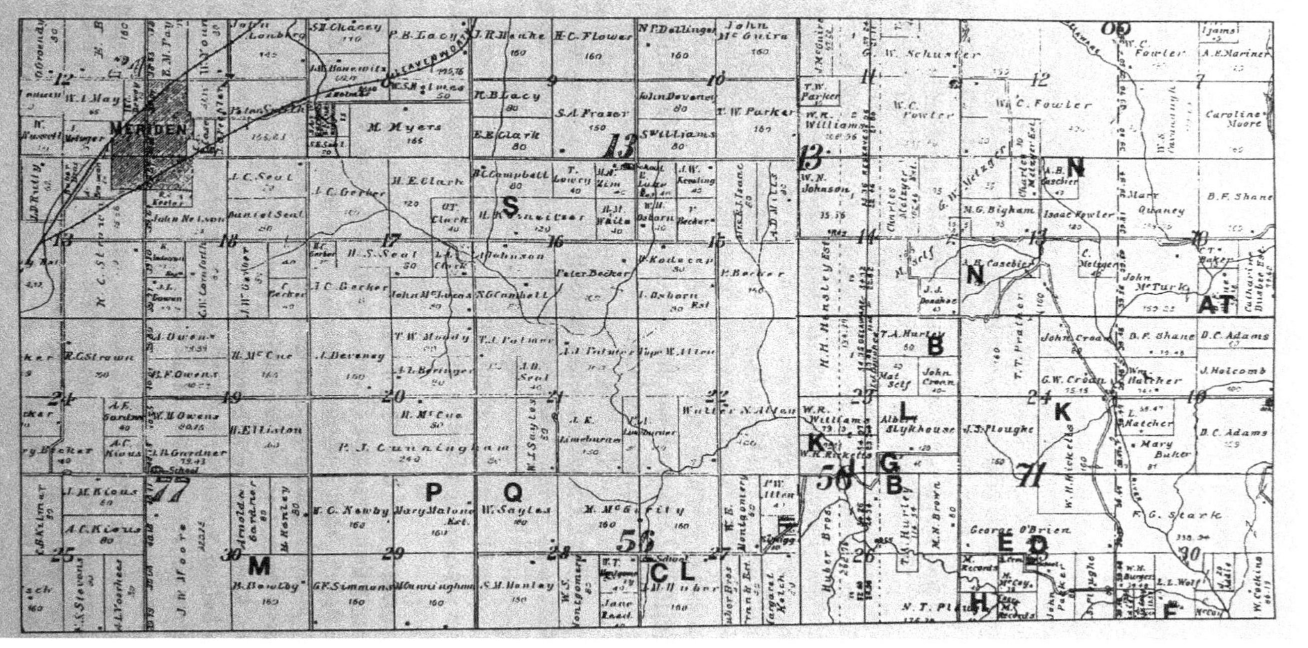

A. T.A. Hurley land, 1865
B. T.A. Hurley farm, 1870-1923
C. Huber schoolhouse
D. Olive Branch schoolhouse
E. Olive Branch Cemetery
F. LL Wolf Country Store
G. Eli Hurley home, ca. 1901
H. E. Hurley rented home, 1910
J. Luie Gardner family, ca. 1897
K. WR Ricketts farm, 1899
L. Ben Bowlby early farm (Nate Isaac's farm just to east)
M. Ben Bowlby farm, 1899
N. AB Casebier, 1899
P. Eli Metzger, 1860
Q. John Metzger Jr., 1860
S. Jacob Metzger, 1861
T. Samuel Metzger, 1865

Acknowledgments

Many people along the way encouraged me as I worked on this project. Lila strongly prodded me, sometimes by postcard or letter, other times over the phone. I hope she somehow knows the book is published and is pleased with the "sweeping saga" that she desired.

I am grateful to my family, especially my two boys. They probably wondered what I was doing, all those many hours when I was tucked away in my office at home.

Along the way, some amazing teachers instilled in me a love for reading and writing. Elizabeth Smith, my favorite grade school teacher and a surrogate grandmother, introduced me to Laura Ingalls Wilder's "Little House" books. Other great encouragers were Bev Olson Buller and Bev Hunter, my middle school and high school English teachers; Tom Averill, my creative writing instructor at Washburn; and Nan Harper and David Dary, who grounded me in reporting and taught me how to write press releases at KU's William Allen White School of Journalism.

My mom, Shirley Hurley, liked to point out that my dad, who had no formal training, became a published author before I did. And then my husband Sam did the same.

To all of these folks, and to anyone who has cheered me on, I give a hearty thanks.

—KHA

Sources

Baptism/marriage records, census records, county courthouse records, death certificates, family genealogy records and maps.

"Flora's Dial," by John Wesley Hanson. Published by Jonathan Allen, Lowell, Mass., and B.B. Mussey, Boston, 1846. 206 pgs.

"From Then to Now," autobiography by Eli Martin Hurley. Dec. 1957. 15 pgs.

Interview with Maude Hurley Funston, ca. 1981.

Interviews with Daryl Becker, Eugene Cook, Gene Cook, Bob McGarity and Charles Myers, ca. 1994.

Lula Gardner Hurley autobiography, Jan. 14, 1957. 10 pgs.

Nellie Hurley Pugh autobiography. 2 pgs.

Nora Hurley Baker autobiography. 3 pgs.

"Ole Nate's Story," Delila Mize McCabe. 34 pgs.

"The Farmhouse Murders," by Richard A. Swallow. 21 pgs.

"Thomas Andrew Hurley, His Descendants, and the Related Families of Metzger and Stout," by Lucius Metzger Hurley and Stanley Steele Funston. 1995. 139 pgs.

"William G. Cutler's History of Kansas," 1883, published by A.T. Andreas, Chicago, Ill.

Many accounts of the tragedy in newspapers, including *The Meriden Ledger, The Oskaloosa Independent, The Topeka Daily Capital* and *The Valley Falls Vindicator.*

"Double Murder Suicide is Solution," *Florence Bulletin,* May 24, 1923, pg. 1.

"Extraordinary Explanation of an 'Unexplainable Murder Mystery, '" American Weekly Inc., magazine insert in *The San Francisco Examiner,* Sun., March 27, 1927, pg. 125.

"Three Burn in Home," *Meriden Message,* May 18, 1923, pg. 4.

"What Has Happened to Justice?" by Peter Levins, *The Atlanta Journal Constitution Magazine,* Sunday, June 7, 1931, pg. 8. (Picked up by "True Detective Tales" syndicate, and published in the *Pittsburgh Sun-Telegraph,* Thursday, Aug. 22, 1940, pg. 13.)

Index

About the Authors

Author, poet and songwriter DELILA MIZE MCCABE was born in Topeka, Kan. She married Charles McCabe in 1938. Five years later, they moved to Meriden, Kan. Together they had three daughters: Jody, Lanny and Chrisie.

McCabe became a certified nurse, served as an in-home care nurse, and later took care of the elderly in the house that she and Charlie built on a hill overlooking Perry Lake, called The Lake Place. She wrote a short story called "Ole Nate's Story," which this book is partly based on, and a book of poetry called "Bushels of Love." McCabe died in 1998 at the age of 78.

KIM HURLEY ANDREWS was born and raised in Newton, Kan. She studied creative writing at Washburn University of Topeka before graduating from The University of Kansas with a bachelor's degree in journalism. Over the next twenty years, Andrews worked as an editor and freelance writer for national consumer and trade publications. She also worked for one of the largest ad agencies in Kansas.

At 43, she answered the call to ministry. In 2017, Andrews received an M.Div. from United Theological Seminary in Dayton, Ohio. She was ordained as an elder by the United Methodist Church in 2023 and has served ten congregations. She is married to Sam Andrews and has two grown sons, Gannon and Dakota. This is her first book.

When the Leaves Began to Unfold:
The Hurley Murder Mystery

www.ingramcontent.com/pod-product-compliance
Lightning Source LLC
LaVergne TN
LVHW010613100826
845148LV00014B/2956
* 9 7 8 0 5 7 8 8 8 9 2 4 5 *